Baby Score

A Second Chance Sports Romance

By: Piper Sullivan

Table of Contents

Chapter 1

All it took was one eventful and memorable night and here I was, a mother with a four-year-old toddler who refused to speak like other children his age and who believed that he had another family. He compared everything I did to his imaginary mother; from the food I gave him to the clothes I dressed him in. He couldn't get himself to even call me mom. But here, where Braden lay sleeping, he looked like a real angel. I just wish I knew why he was so different from other children. Everything went for a loop after his second birthday. Initially I assumed it was the terrible-two phase all experts refer to when it came to toddler behaviour, but two years later I wasn't all that sure. He became progressively worse as he got older and I had no idea how to help him. Every day he would talk about his other mother, the one who died a horrible death after being attacked by white tigers, and his little sister who fell into the ice. And if I dared tell him that it's his imagination he would throw the worst temper tantrums ever. He believed everything his mind conjured up, it was so real for him that he would spend hours crying about his dead mother and how he couldn't help his little sister.

"Is he sleeping?" Damien whispered from the doorway.

If it wasn't for my brother I would be so lost, but I had to start accepting the fact that Damien would soon move away to start his own family.

"Yeah finally, I just wish I knew what triggered him to behave this way," I said softly while I brushed the brown curls away from Braden's forehead.

"Maybe you should consider taking him to a paediatrician or a child psychologist," Damien suggested.

"And tell them that my child believes I'm not his mother?" I piped up and laughed softly, "I mean really, white tigers? Just today he told me how he used to walk in knee deep snow to go collect fire wood for his family, I honestly have no idea where all this comes from."

Damien came to stand next to me and placed his hand on my shoulder, "You're going to have to get some expert advice Rae, otherwise you'll never figure it out. This behaviour is not normal."

No shit Sherlock, of course it's not normal, "I'll make an appointment to get him assessed, but I'm just so scared they find something horribly wrong with him."

I swallowed at the lump in my throat, choking back the tears of defeat. What if my son was odd, what if he was diagnosed with some mental disorder that required permanent care that would eventually result in him never having a normal childhood? The questions were endless. I spent many nights researching all possibilities, from past life experiences to Autism and Schizophrenia, but all that resulted in, was me going more insane every day.

"It will only help you Rae and once you know what's going on, you will be better equipped to deal with these challenges. You should also consider getting in touch with Caleb; he has the right to know."

"Caleb? Why would I do that?" I asked shocked, I never told anyone that Caleb was Braden's father.

"I wasn't born yesterday. You two were close, hell, you were almost inseparable. And when you came with the news about your pregnancy, I knew straight away."

Wow, and he kept quiet all this time? "Why did you never say anything?"

"I figured you'll talk when the time was right, which never happened. But still, you need to get in touch with him."

Maybe my brother was right, Caleb had the right to know, but how on earth was I going to find him? The last I heard he was in the military, who knows where he was now. And if I did find him what do I tell him? *Oh by the way, you left and I was pregnant. Congratulations you're a dad.*

"I wouldn't even know where to find him Damien, it's been five years. The day he left, he left for good," I said and pushed myself up off the floor and walked out of Braden's room pulling the door closed behind me.

"I have his number; maybe you should just give him a call, test the waters and see how he is. In a week I'm leaving and if you ask me you are going to need all support you can get. Doing this on your own will be no easy task," he said and hugged me tight.

I was going to miss Damien once he was gone. Over the past few years, he had been my pillar of strength. He was the only one who understood me and even more so, he was the closest thing to a father Braden ever had. The idea of him leaving was almost too much to bear. I couldn't even bring myself to tell Braden.

After Damien left, I flopped down on the sofa and finally broke down. This was the only time I could allow my own weaknesses to surface knowing that no-one was around to witness them. I had to stay strong, for Braden. Sometimes when I was caught up in my own thoughts, I felt like the protagonist in my own stage play with the world as the audience. But rather than cheering me on, they flung rotten tomatoes and lettuce at me.

I reached for my phone and scrolled down the list of contacts, compared to how many friends I had back in college to the handful I had now, I was nothing short of being a recluse who avoided social media like the black plague and hid behind books and manuscripts to avoid meeting new people. I paused at Caleb's name, Damien must have added him to my address book when I wasn't looking, I realized and my thumb hovered over the message icon.

"Mommy!" it was Braden's hysterical cry that sounded from the bedroom and I immediately dropped my phone to run to his side.

"Mommy's here sweetheart," I said trying to pull him into my arms.

"No! Mommy, I want my mommy!"

He was looking for his imaginary mom again and this was the third time in one day this episode repeated itself.

"She's not real Braden," I said trying my best not to over react and show him that I'm upset.

"Mommy!" he kept on as if he didn't hear a word I just said.

Okay, calm down Rae, just go with it, I told myself and closed my eyes then let Braden go. He flopped down on the bed and in one motion rolled onto the floor kicking and screaming. Tears stung my eyes as I tried to keep my wits about myself, but it wasn't easy.

All I was left to do was lie down on the bed and watch him eventually cry himself to sleep. As soon as he was asleep I got up and pulled a blanket over his small frame. Exhausted I decided to stay in his room and finally fell asleep on his bed.

Chapter 2

Caleb

I was ready as ever, adrenalin pumping through my veins as sweat dripped down my face. All we needed was one drop kick over the posts and we would win this game and walk away as the undefeated champions to win the Inaugural Season. I glanced at the clock –seventy eight minutes and counting. The ball came flying my way and I caught it mid-air, and without a second thought I drop kicked the ball and sent it sailing right between the goal posts. The sound of the crowds as they cheered was one of the best feelings any rugby player could ever experience. It was a sense of achievement.

The final whistle blew and the game was set with the Denver Stampede winning by 39 to 33 against the Ohio Aviators, it was a close one to say the least, but we did it.

After the game, instead of joining the guys for a night out to celebrate our victory, I headed home. Despite the excitement that still flowed through my veins I felt irritable and the text from Damien did not help at all. That was a part of my life I laid to rest a long time ago. Why on earth did he think I wanted to touch base with Rae? The last time I saw her was the day I left to do my civil duty for my country and I never looked back again. Surely she finally settled down with someone who was able to give her what her heart desired.

I gritted my teeth, fighting off the sudden ache that emitted from my chest, we had a good thing going, but we were still so young. And after my father decided that my mother wasn't good enough for him and he hooked up with miss-priss, I realized then and there that love was nothing but a pain in the arse. It was an overrated emotion that just brought pain and disappointment. It was the one thing I would never forget. The look on my mother's face when my dad arrived home with Leandra on his arm as if she was stuck to him like an appendage. If he could have his way he would have opted for a polygamous lifestyle, one where he could have multiple wives and father a multitude of children, but then again he didn't care much for children. I knew that.

I dropped my duffle bag on the ground and went straight for the bourbon; I needed something strong to calm the anger that raged deep in my soul. I'll sleep off this sudden annoying feeling and wake up in top form, ready for the ride up-country. My ass and fingers itched to get on my bike and just be one with it and be free.

I was about to settle down when my phone rang, it was Joanne a most welcome distraction at the best of times.

"Hey babe," I said answering the phone and just as I thought she wanted to hook up again. The convenience of being in the national rugby squad was that women, more specifically cheer leaders would throw themselves at you shamelessly without expecting the strings that usually come as part and parcel of any relationship.

"I'm having an early night, but why don't you come around over the weekend and we can head out to the club?"

There was an evident disappointment that lingered in her tone, and as much as I needed a distraction, I wasn't really in the mood for company.

"Why don't you send me a teaser, and I can keep it as a reminder of what to expect when I see you again," I suggested with a smirk.

I didn't need to do any convincing on my part, she was more than willing to share the occasional sneak peek that most men could only dream of seeing, but even though I asked for it, I knew it would do nothing to any part of my anatomy.

I finally killed the call after she tried again to convince me to see her and told her that I will only be back in town by the weekend.

***

The morning arrived with promise and regardless of my bourbon induced hangover I knew that once I was on my motorbike it would disappear instantly. A long hard ride would also silence my conscience that kept nagging me to call Rae. The past was just that – past tense – it had no place in my future. Past experience taught me that valuable lesson. The moment you allow the past to command your future you may as well kiss your ass goodbye.

I clicked the remote and the garage door slowly rolled open. There it stood in all its glory, my Harley Davidson, chrome polished frame and its complimentary blue and diamond ice finish. It was nothing short of a majestic piece of machinery that made me crave the open road. My leathers crunched against the leather seat and as I started her up she became an extension of my own body.

I finally hit the open road and opened the throttle, and as the wind whipped past me I could sense the different aromas as they passed me by. It was never the same, each time I rode my bike it was new smells and sounds that kept me alert. But unlike other times where it was just me and my bike, Rae's face kept flashing in my mind's eye.

That last day before I left for the military, there was a sadness in her eyes, it was as if she knew I was never coming back and although I didn't explicitly tell her or break up with her, she sensed it. When I was out on detail, I received two letters from her and I never responded to either one. For days after her first letter to me, I contemplated the future, trying to figure out where she fitted into my life. By the time I got the second letter, I was elbow deep in desert sand fighting for a cause bigger than my own and time simply won. It was the time to let go, let go of the past so that I could work on my own uncertain future. I never intended on looking back, until now.

Chapter 3

Raedene

I hated doctors' rooms like I hate creamed spinach, the smell of disinfectant always reminded me of death, but I had no choice. Damien insisted I seek help to try and figure out what was wrong with Braden. Scattered magazines lay across the table in the waiting room; next to us was an old man whose face mapped the years of hardship he must have endured in his life time. I couldn't help but wonder what brought him here today.

"Miss Callaway, you can come through," the receptionist said, standing with our file in her hand.

I reached out to take Braden's hand, but as usual he pulled away and my heart sank. *This was going to be interesting.*

We spent close on an hour with the psychologist, who made Braden draw pictures of his family. It was no surprise when he drew his imaginary family, a mother with long brown hair, a dad he had never mentioned before and a little sister, all standing next to what looked to be a wooden house covered in snow. I didn't even feature. After all the tests were done, Braden was left to play in the play room while I waited for the conclusion to this madness.

"Miss Callaway, does Braden have a father?" he asked and I cringed.

"Well, it's complicated, I only found out I was pregnant after his dad was out of the picture, so he doesn't know his dad."

"Have you ever told him about his dad?"

"No, he never asks about him, he has also never mentioned his imaginary dad," I said, watching him jot down notes.

Why did I suddenly feel like I was under scrutiny?

"Look, it's very early to tell, and there are other tests I can run, but from what I am able to determine, it looks like Braden is experiencing some sort of past life regression, are you familiar with that term?"

Off course I am, I wasn't born under a rock, "Yes I am, but as far as I know that's a lot of speculation with no real facts to prove that it actually exist."

"Yes, it is. The idea of past life regression is unfortunately unchartered territory, but some great progress has been made to determine the science behind it," he slid a brochure over to me and then smiled, "Children eventually grow out of it. With the right approach, they soon learn that the past life they tend to cling to is something of the past and they soon start to adopt their new life with much enthusiasm."

"Okay, so what am I supposed to do now? I mean, he hardly talks and putting him in a day care makes it even worse, because other kids make fun of him."

"It's no easy task, but I would like to help you through the process," he said and rode back in his chair.

"I don't want him on any medication," I objected, that was the last thing I wanted. Nowadays everyone seems to want to shove pills down kids' throats for the simplest of conditions. If the kid is too active its ADHD, when all it is, is the fact that the child has no way of expending the pent-up energy that gathers from spending too much time behind the television or playing computer games.

"No pills. Your first step is to stop rejecting his other family, you need to embrace them. Ask him to tell you about them. You need to show him that you are interested in his life, and that you care for his other family."

What he said made perfect sense; I was just not so sure if I could cope with the jealousy factor. Braden compared me to his mom with everything I did.

"Another thing I might suggest is to get in touch with his biological father if you can. Giving him that closure might just trigger him, the fact that he has never mentioned that to you means that he is afraid to approach the subject with you."

"I'll see what I can do, it's no easy task to get in touch with his father, but I'll try."

That was it, settled. I left the rooms with an information overload and a threatening migraine; at least it wasn't anything serious like Autism, which was a relief. Now all I needed to do was figure out how I was going to reach out to my little champ.

Much later that day after taking pain killers and while Braden was taking his afternoon nap, I picked up the pamphlet the doctor gave me. *Lamarckism* - a condition whereby an organism passes on acquired characteristics to offspring, which may include past memories of the parents or grandparents. The more I read the more I realized that going to the psychologist wasn't such a bad idea after all. There were still a lot of questions that remained unanswered and the condition itself was still being studied in-depth, but at least I had some direction now.

Get in touch with his biological father – my conscience reminded me very inaptly. Caleb had no idea that Braden existed, how was I ever going to tell him after all these years?

Chapter 4

Caleb

I shoved the empty glass over to the bar tender and around me the bar was buzzing with bikers from all over taking advantage of happy hour. Above me the television blared out loud, as always baseball or football, never rugby.

"How about changing the channel," I asked the bartender above the noise.

"Watcha wanna watch?" he asked, leaning on the counter with his greasy elbow.

"Rugby," I said blankly, hoping that it may be a much-needed distraction from the thoughts that haunted me.

"Naw man, no-one watches that backwards ball passing shit," he said laughing and shook his head enough to make his double chin quiver like a blob of jelly.

Exactly the response I expected, these morons all lived under a rock of their own, each with shields on either side of their eyes. Talk about one track minded dumbasses. This dump was seriously starting to work on my nerves.

"Hey Caleb, wanna play a game of pool?"

It was Stinger, who called me over and under normal circumstances I would never turn down the challenge to beat him at pool, but it wasn't going to help my predicament. I just couldn't get Rae out of my mind.

"No I'm good, I'm going to head out anyway," I said and stood up to put on my leather jacket, "I have an early morning tomorrow," lame excuse, I know, but there wasn't much else I could say.

On my way, out I greeted the guys from a bikers' club that frequent the place and headed out. The cool night air was a total contrast to the musty dank smell of the bar. I took a moment just to breathe it in and chase away the smell of cigar smoke that clung to my nostrils. When I closed my eyes, an image of Rae popped into my head. She had the cutest button nose with a dust of freckles that shaded her nose and cheeks, which she hated, but I always told her that she had them because she was kissed by the sun. And she ever did cut her long silky red hair as she always threatened to do on hot summer days. For a moment, I could almost feel her hair threading through my fingers. I recalled the last night we spent together at her dorm room; I had to climb up the side of the dormitory to avoid being caught by the matron on duty. That night was imprinted in my mind forever. She had this cute blush that made her look all innocent while she slowly undressed. I was like a horny teenager then, she never got past her bra, I simply couldn't wait to touch her, and boy did I touch her! She was like clay in a potter's hand, and I was the potter, moulding her body with my hands and my lips.

I let out a groan and shook my head; these were careless memories that evoked nothing but pain and loss. I was about to get back on my bike when my phone vibrated in my pocket, it was a message from an unknown number, but the message was from no stranger.

Hey Caleb, it's been a while, where are you these days? Rae

We'll I'll be damned, Damien must have given her my number, how else would she have gotten it? I read her text again, my thumb hovering over the reply button, but instead I locked my phone and shoved it back in my pocket. Do I reply to her or do I ignore the text? If I had to be outright honest with myself, there was no place in my world for a woman, not one I would settle down with anyway. My life was an easy cruise, I had everything I wanted. I played the game I loved; I got to go on road trips without anyone tying me down. I was pretty damn comfortable and the best part was that money was no problem. My father's business was self-sustaining with board members running it expertly and all I had to do was show up at meetings and rake in the benefits of being the main shareholder. Besides that, I had Hayley, Stephanie, Joanne and Tracy the four hottest cheerleaders of our squad who were more than willing to be content with one night stands when the mood was right. What else could I possibly ask for?

By the time I got home my fingers were frozen and my face was numb, but in my pocket my phone was like a burning coal, reminding me of Rae's text. I rushed inside, tore off my jacket and rolled my shoulders to relieve some tension. What was it with me, and why was she contacting me now after all these years, surely she wasn't still looking for closure.

I looked at her text again and against my better judgement I hit reply.

Hey, I'm in Denver living the life, you? C.

I didn't quite expect such a quick reply, but there it was.

I'm in Lafayette, we're neighbours, fancy that!

I could hardly stand the suspense, there was more to this than idle chit chat, so instead of responding by text I called.

There was a slight delay in her answering her phone, and I was about to hang up when a tentative *hello* resonated on the other side.

"I hope you don't mind me calling you," I said and as lowered myself down on the sofa toeing my boots off.

"Oh no, not at all, it was a little unexpected, that's all," she said, she sounded different. Obviously four years down the line I couldn't exactly expect her to sound the same, but I did notice that there was sadness in her tone.

"Is everything okay?"

"Yeah, of course it is..." a suspended pause followed, "well, no. There's something I need to talk to you about."

"I gathered as much after Damien told me to call you, so what's up?" I asked and for some reason the thought of her getting married popped up in my mind. I felt my mood change from indifference to annoyance. Why would her getting married affect me this way after all these years? I shifted and stuffed another cushion under my head. I had no reason to be upset in fact I should be happy for her.

"Caleb, I-I don't know how to say this..." she started.

"You're getting married, is that it?" I butted in.

"What? No!" she said in a high-pitched tone followed by a soft controlled sigh, "maybe this was a mistake, I need to go."

Without as much as a goodbye she hung up and I stared blankly at my phone. I wanted to call her back but the uneasy feeling that settled in the pit of my stomach made me think twice. Instead of calling her back, I shoved my phone in my pocket and got on my bike again. Maybe she was right, it *was* a mistake and repeating history had the habit of stabbing you in the back. I much preferred to let sleeping dogs lie.

Chapter 5

Rae

What was I thinking considering telling Caleb about Braden after all these years? Caleb had gone on with his life, and I was sure that the last thing he would expect is a surprise father's-day gift. To suddenly throw a spanner in the works for him could have serious implications. What if he was married or planning to get married, what would his wife or fiancée do or say? The thought of him being married caught me by surprise as a sudden stab of pain poked at my insides, but the moment it surfaced I was quick to supressed it with a dose of reality.

All these years, I managed quite fine on my own and if it wasn't for Braden's imaginary world, I would not be in this predicament in the first place, in fact, I wouldn't even have considered calling him at all. I looked down at Braden where he sat playing with his Legos and I couldn't help but smile, when he was like this he was so easy to handle and these were the times I wish I could just reach out and hug him and never let him go. Just as I moved to sit on the floor with Braden and attempt to play with him, my phone rang, and when I saw the caller ID my heart skipped a beat. It was Caleb. He wasn't going to let it go, was he?

"Hello," I answered tentatively.

"Hey, I figured you needed time to gather yourself after my call last night," he said and paused, "You wanted to tell me something?"

"It was nothing," I lied.

"Are you kidding me? After five years, you call to tell me something and then get cold feet?"

I went quiet, and I could hear Caleb breathing on the other end, maybe it was time to come clean and this was a cosmic sign to speak my mind once and for all.

"I have a, well actually, we have a son, he's four years old now and his name is Braden."

You know that feeling you get when it feels as if your entire world just got sucked into a black hole and everything faded into the shadows of uncertainty leaving you with nothing but the unexpected truth staring you right in the face? No, me neither and why? Because I knew that the moment I told Caleb he was a father, it will undeniably change the past, present and the future. That was the exact magnitude of this weighted situation. I bet you Caleb had his entire life mapped out; from the coffee he drank every morning to the toothpaste he'd been using since I first met him. And this was the last thing he would have expected, and by the deadly silence that followed, I knew that he was not going to take lightly to the news.

"I'm sorry? Did you just say I have a son?" he sounded tentative.

"Yes, his name is Braden, he's four now."

"Send me your address, I'm sending my driver to pick you up," he demanded and by the tone of his voice, I couldn't quite determine if he was angry, sad or excited.

"You're sending your driver?"

I should have figured, even with all that went down when his dad walked out on him; he still had the luxuries most other people could only dream of.

"Yes, my driver. Since I have a son I would very much like to see him," he stated, a little too expressively.

"I know you do, but there are things I need to tell you first..."

"It can wait, make sure you're packed and ready, now can I please have your address?"

I rambled off my address and then we ended the call.

This was not going to be a walk in the park; I could tell by his tone that he was upset, if not upset at least irritated. What surprised me even more was that he simply accepted it. I would have expected him to at least question my intensions, but instead he simply arranged for his driver to collect me.

Chapter 6

Caleb

I stared down at the small piece of paper I scribbled Rae's address down on; my mind was still spinning like an out of control gear on a lawnmower. All this time and she never bothered to let me know I had a son. Expecting her to be married and dealing with my own disappointment was one thing, finding out that I'm a dad was a whole different ball game. It was like throwing me into a tennis game expecting me to know what I'm doing.

I dragged my fingers through my hair and sank down on the sofa. The why's and if's all started to fight a territorial battle in my mind all at once. The overwhelming realization that I was a father was almost too surreal.

I grabbed my phone again and dialled Damien, he had some serious explaining to do, I would have expected my best friend to at least give me some warning.

"Hey, so I assume you spoke to Rae?" Damien said straight off the bat and it instantly annoyed me.

"Bro, seriously, you knew that I was a dad and never bothered to tell me?" I ground out as I paced up and down.

"It wasn't my place to tell you, she's my sister and besides, it was only a hunch I had all this time, she only admitted it to me when I told you to get in touch with her again."

The thing with Damien was that he was painfully in control of any situation even at the worst of times. By the tone of his voice he didn't sound intimidated or upset, he sounded as if he rehearsed this for a public speech to convince people that radioactive waste was safe.

"Bullshit! You knew this all along and if you had told me about this back when we were in the military, I would have tried to at least be supportive of Rae, and I would have had a chance to get to know my own son."

"I swear to you, I didn't know. She never even told our parents you were the father."

"For fuck sakes man, I have no idea how to raise a son," I admitted and pinched the bridge of my nose.

"So you're planning on raising Braden?"

"No, yes, I mean, I have no idea. I've sent Samson to go fetch them and bring them to Denver, I honestly have no idea what to expect."

"A word of advice, they are both fragile, especially Braden so try and stay calm. Things will work themselves out."

What did he mean by *fragile*, was Rae in some sort of trouble?

"Fragile, how?"

"That my friend, you will soon figure out, all I'm asking is that you take the time to listen to Rae," he said. But I wasn't so sure if I could be tamed after finding out that the mother of my child had kept him hidden from me as if he was a dirty secret.

"I can't promise you that, but I'll try," I said and then hung up.

There were so many secrets all of a sudden, and I had no idea how to handle it. In my world, it was a matter of black and white. You tackle the player; you steal the ball you score a tri. There were no grey areas, but now I was facing a million shades of grey all at the same time.

Chapter 7

Raedene

Everything just happened so fast, by nine o'clock the next morning a Lexus pulled up in front of the house and good old Samson got out and opened the door for us. Some things never change; I can still remember him being dropped off at college by Samson. Caleb was always the spoiled, rich kid amongst the rest of us. Things did however change drastically after his parents' divorce, and for some reason I figured that he may have finally descended by force of gravity and tasted real-life after he left for the military.

"Miss Callaway, it's lovely to see you again," Samson greeted me with a friendly smile.

"Hi Samson, it's been a while hasn't it?"

"Indeed. And I see your little boy looks just like you," he commented.

It was true, Braden had my strawberry blonde hair and forest green eyes, but on closer inspection the shape of his mouth and nose was a cloned copy of Caleb's.

"Yes he has my eyes, but that's about it." *Did Samson know that Braden was Caleb's son?* Unsure of what Caleb had confided in his old friend, I omitted to mention the resemblances between the two.

The closer we got to Denver the more nervous I became, so much so that I could feel a hollow form in the pit of my stomach. The last time I was this nervous was when I found out I was pregnant. It was like yesterday when I looked at the two pink lines on the pregnancy test, and now I had no idea how I was going to explain to Caleb why I never told him.

As we turned into the driveway through the large automated gates I wanted to run. He really outdid himself this time. The house looked like a glorified bachelor pad with a masterful modern cubed design and large windows. It was nothing short of a glass house apart from the concrete and wood that panelled the sides, definitely not designed for a family or kids. Not that I was actually hoping to rekindle an old flame, frankly there was nothing left to rekindle.

To make matters worse, Caleb was standing outside on the stairs, legs apart and his arms folded across his chest. Completely transformed, he was much bulkier in his biceps and chest than I remember. The frown that furrowed between his brows was intimidating and for a moment I contemplated asking Samson to take me back home. If it wasn't for Braden, I probably would have been gone by now.

Caleb reached the car and opened the door for us and I attempted a casual smile, I could feel the muscles in my cheeks jump uncomfortably and I quickly pursed my lips to relieve the tension.

"I'm glad you decided to come," he said without a smile but glanced right past me at Braden who was still fast asleep on the back seat.

You didn't really give me a choice, I thought to say, but instead I nodded, "It wasn't too much trouble."

Samson brought our luggage and came to stand beside me and Caleb's frown deepened, "Is that all you have with you?"

What did he expect, it wasn't as if I was moving in, "Yes, it's just a weekend bag, it's enough for a couple of days."

I saw the muscle jump in his jaw as he clenched his mouth shut, clearly holding back whatever he wanted to say.

"Samson will take your stuff upstairs; will you be okay to carry him or can I take him?" he asked hesitantly.

"No it's fine, I'll take him," I quickly said and ducked into the car pulling Braden closer and lifting him into my arms.

"Are you sure? He looks a little heavy."

"I'm used to it and I don't want him to wake up in a stranger's arms," I said and immediately wished I had a filter.

The pain that flashed in Caleb's eyes was evident, and I instantly felt terrible. Although he was technically a stranger to Braden, he was still his dad and it wasn't exactly his fault that he never had part in his son's life.

"Actually, my back is hurting a little, so if you don't mind carrying him that will be great."

I carefully placed Braden in Caleb's arms and as his hand brushed my arm I felt that familiar spark that shot through every fibre of my being and from the look in his eyes, he felt it too. I clumsily took a step back and he abruptly turned away and headed into the house. I waited outside for a few minutes to calm the raging storm inside me. I was halfway up the stairs when my heart stopped, I could have sworn I heard Braden's voice and as I entered the open plan living room I stopped. Caleb was sitting on a small square bench with Braden next to him looking through a state of the art telescope. I literally clutched the front of my shirt trying to calm myself down since it felt as if my heart was about to jump out of my chest.

"Now if you turn this knob just a little to the left it increases the focus ratio. Can you see the craters on the moon now?" Caleb asked Braden.

"I can!" Braden said excitedly, "Is there really a man on the moon?"

"I think there is buddy, but he hides so well. Maybe one day we'll be able to see him."

Oh dear god, Braden was having a conversation with Caleb, how was that even possible? Braden hardly spoke to me other than when he needed food, or water. Tears stung my eyes, I felt like a complete failure as a mother.

"Miss Callaway, can I show you to your room?"

Samson appeared next to me just in time to save me from a completely breakdown. I glanced at Caleb and he nodded, that was my cue. And with a heavy heart and a lump in my throat, I followed Samson.

Chapter 8

Caleb

For a moment before Rae arrived I had doubts about Braden. I couldn't help but wonder if he was really mine, but when I laid eyes on him as Rae placed him in my arms, all the doubt I harboured disappeared. He may have her hair and eyes but he definitely had my features. And now sitting here with him looking at the moon, even if it was broad daylight, it felt as if my heart was about to explode in my chest. He was such a bright little boy regardless of the sadness in his eyes.

I spent most of the day catching up with Braden, who told me the strangest story of his mother and sister, but I assumed it was his imagination running away with him so I simply played along. He spoke of them with such conviction that he could make me believe they were real.

Later that evening after he was settled down and was sleeping peacefully, I waited for Rae to join me for dinner. Naturally I had completely forgotten that I had a date with a friend and when the doorbell rang I cursed inwardly and rushed to do damage control.

"Hey handsome, you ready to go?" Joanne said as she sauntered into the house.

"Hey, I'm kind of in the middle of something, I had unexpected guests that arrived a little while ago, can we do this another time?" I asked uncomfortably.

"Oh please, no need to hide your guests from me, we can just stay in and order some dinner."

She was relentless, and the only reason I kept her company was because she was hot. It was all about the ego if I was honest.

"It's a little complicated, but I'll call you tomorrow and explain everything," I said modestly, walking her out the door.

"Caleb?" I closed my eyes and took a deep breath. *Shit*.

"Oh who's that?" Joanne asked and peeked over my shoulder.

"No-one," I said and took her by her arm.

"Caleb, Braden is awake and he's looking for you..." Rae started and then grew silent.

"I'll be right up," I said as Joanne pushed past me.

Great! Just what I needed, I turned to Rae and stepped aside, "Rae, this is Joanne, Joanne, this is Rae, she's here with her son for the weekend," the daggers that shot from Rae's eyes did not go unnoticed, and I quickly corrected myself, "I mean with our son, so I'll give you a call tomorrow."

The way Joanne raised her brows was nothing but arrogant and to top it off, she looked Rae up and down as if she was something that the cat dragged in. I'm not going to lie, but Joanne lacked the humble-factor. And right now, I just needed her gone.

By comparison Rae was everything Joanne wasn't. She was beautiful in a natural kind of way, she didn't plaster her face with makeup thick enough to scrape off with a spatula, and she was naturally shaped, unlike the overly thin women that hang out in the locker rooms waiting to bait the unsuspecting sport stars with their glamor and haughty attitudes. My chest tightened when Rae disappeared around the corner, but at the same time relief flooded me when Joanne spun around on her heels and stormed down the stairs back to her car. At least that settled it, I only had one woman to contend with at this point, and Joanne was hardly intimidating. In no time, she would be moving on to her next victim like a praying mantis and I'll be nothing but a memory.

I found Rae outside at the pool when I finally conjured up the courage to talk to her.

"You didn't have to walk away, Joanne was leaving anyway," I said as I came to sit on the lounger next to her.

"It's none of my business, you can entertain whoever you want, it's your house," she said laying back and closing her eyes.

"I know that," I said trying not to let my irritation surface, "But if you haven't noticed, I just found out I am a father; it's a lot of information to process, so I didn't feel like other company. Why after all these years did you only contact me now?"

She draped her arm over her eyes and sighed, "When you left to join the military I didn't expect to see you again, I waited for a letter or a phone call every day, and when you didn't contact me I closed that chapter of my life,"

Perhaps I could have made some effort, but still there was no excuse for her to keep the pregnancy from me, "I know I could have written but I was dealing with a lot of shit, you know that."

"I do, and I was also dealing with a lot. I found out I was pregnant, Damien had no idea where you were stationed, and I had no way of contacting you. Time went by too quickly to figure out how to find you."

"So why now?"

She sat up and looked at me; her eyes were glistening with tears.

"Braden is a troubled child. Damien and the psychologist suggested I contact you since it may help him get better," she started to say and I felt the sting of disappointment linger at the realization that if circumstances were any different, I would still be oblivious to my own son's existence. But Damien's words to me reminded me to listen to her and instead of voicing my own opinion I rubbed my forehead and gave her time to continue.

She told me all about Braden and his past life regression, which explained the stories he told me. It was a strange one to say the least, how on earth was I going to help him with all that. She rambled on, finally telling me that the psychologist suggested that she introduces Braden to me since he lacks the much-needed father figure in his life.

"So let me get this straight, if he was normal, you would never have contacted me?"

"This is not about us Caleb, it's about our son, he needs help, and the psychologist suggested I find you. We parted ways on bad terms a long time ago; surely you didn't expect me to just fall over my feet to find you?"

"No I didn't but I reckon a child is a pretty big thing," I objected.

"You think I don't know that? *Love is a sham,* you said, *it's something I can live without,* you said, *I never want kids,* you said. Pray-tell what did you expect me to do with all that?"

I stood up and cracked my knuckles, how dare she hold that against me. I was bloody pissed that day when my dad decided to leave my mom for someone only five years older than me. Those words were said in anger.

"People say things in anger when they are hurt. You can't be that ignorant that you would think I really meant what I said," I said raising my voice just a fraction.

"Your silence spoke volumes, thank you very much," she retorted and stood up shoving me out of the way, but as she stepped, she lost her footing and tumbled into the pool.

I didn't think twice before I too jumped in, clothes and all. Instinctively I gathered her in my arms; knowing she had a phobia for water ever since her near drowning incident when she was only six.

But instead of accepting my help she pushed at my chest and swam to the corner of the pool.

"I'm not an invalid, I can swim," she spluttered and held unto the edge of the pool.

"Since when? The last time I recalled you hated water," I said and swam towards her.

"I got over all that."

I couldn't help but find her little outburst adorable, and despite everything that had happened, I wanted her, right here right now. Not even the cold water in the pool could constrict the blood flow down south.

I slipped my arm around her waist turning her to face me. Her green eyes were wide and although uncertainty lingered behind the windows of her soul I could see that somewhere in that chaos was the affection I used to see when we were young and in love. Although I had no intentions of settling down soon, the fact remained, I still wanted her and as I dropped my head and captured her lips I let out an audible groan. To my disappointment it was short lived. At first she didn't protest, she opened her lips and our tongues swept over each other's but in a split second she pulled away and hastily lifted herself out of the pool and fled into the house, leaving a nothing but a watery trail behind her.

Maybe it was for the best; attempting anything more would just complicate matters. I had a comfortable life, a big enough bank balance to support her and Braden for the rest of their lives.

"Keep it simple," I said to myself before lifting myself out of the pool.

Chapter 9

Raedene

I was a complete mess after that kiss a few days ago. Especially knowing that it would have been so easy to give in to Caleb, but I just couldn't. I may have known him years ago, but so much time had passed from then to now. And although I may not have paid attention to the sport headlines it soon dawned on me that he was somewhat of a rugby celebrity and that was just a little too overwhelming. Having long overstayed my welcome according to me, myself and I, I was desperate to get back home, but Caleb was making it practically impossible for me to budge. He spent nearly every day with Braden and watching my son blossom like a real four-year-old was worth the torture I had to endure. Okay fine, it wasn't exactly torture, it was worse. It was self-inflicted stupidity. I pussy footed around Caleb all the time, sometimes sneaking around like a mouse in a cattery, expecting to be pounced on any moment. All things considered, one thing was certain, we were not leaving any time soon and since we might as well get comfortable I was going to have to make a trip to town and stock up on clothes and other necessities.

I quickly tied my hair in an untidy bun and made my way downstairs to find Samson. As I reached the bottom of the staircase, the doorbell rang, it was just past eight o'clock in the morning and curiosity got the better of me, especially when Caleb came stalking past me, so I quickly snuck into the kitchen and stood listening.

"What do you want?" Caleb said sounding irritated, which was nothing out of the ordinary, but when the visitor spoke I froze.

"Mr Hayes, is it true that you have an illegitimate child that you only found out about now?"

"It's none of your business," I heard him say in threatening tone.

"Will you be claiming custody of your son?"

There were a few clicking sounds that undoubtedly belonged to a camera. How on earth did they know about Braden? *Joanne* – brilliant, just brilliant, she was a real piece of work.

"I said, it's none of your business, get out before I have you forcibly removed."

"Will you be marrying Miss Callaway?"

"I said get the hell out of here, Miss Callaway and her son has nothing to do with you!" he shouted and this time I heard the door bang shut – Miss Callaway and *her* son – he didn't even acknowledge Braden as his. As I turned around Braden was standing behind me rubbing his eyes.

"Rae I'm thirsty," he said in a croaky voice, and as usual calling me by my first name, but I was so used to it that it hardly bothered me anymore. I simply picked him up in my arms and lifted him unto the kitchen counter.

"Come here sweetheart; let me get you some water, what do you say we go out and get some ice cream later?" I said and gave him a glass of water. I had to get out of here, get some distance between Caleb and I, and I needed to clear my head.

"Is Uncle Caleb going too?" he asked.

"I think he's a little busy today, we won't be out long," I said and took the cup from him.

"I want him to go with," Braden insisted with a pouty lip.

"Not today," I said which only aggravated the situation.

Braden started kicking his legs and wailing about wanting Caleb to go with and nothing I did or say could calm him down. I was about to storm out of the kitchen when Caleb appeared next to me.

"Did I hear ice cream?" he asked and just like that Braden calmed down.

Oh my god, I hate you! "I wanted to take Braden out for ice cream and let you have some time to yourself," I said blankly turning my back to them.

"Why don't I order pizza and ice cream and we can stay here," he suggested instead and I instantly had my back up.

"So you can hide us from the vultures?" I bit out coldly.

"Rae..."

"Don't you Rae me! You couldn't even admit that Braden was..." I started but bit back my words. I couldn't very well drop the bomb on Braden that Caleb was his dad, "Forget it, order pizza. I have things to go do, so if you could watch Braden for the morning that would be great."

I kissed Braden on his forehead and smiled at him, "Caleb will spend the morning with you, mommy has to go and do a few things."

Braden's eyes lit up and my heart sank. He really loved spending time with Caleb; I just wish he would open up to me like he did to his dad.

I didn't even look at Caleb, I simply walked out to find Samson and see if he could take me to town, I was in desperate need of good old fashioned retail therapy.

Chapter 10

Raedene

I stayed out most of the day, and only returned much later that afternoon when the sun was already setting. Throughout the day I kept checking my phone for a message from Caleb, but it never came. I knew that he would have called if things were getting too much and as much as it killed me I had to force myself not to run home and cuddle Braden. I had to simply let the two of them bond. When I got back to the house, both Caleb and Braden were asleep on a bed of pillows in front of the TV, pizza boxes scattered on the floor and game controls haphazardly lying next to them.

I gathered the pizza boxes and quietly went through to the kitchen. Caleb connected with Braden unlike anyone else, for the first time my son was doing things other boys his age did, instead of sitting in the corner of his room reminiscing about his imaginary family. If I had to take this away from him he would be devastated. But staying here would do my heart an injustice. I may still have feelings for Caleb, but I highly doubted he felt the same. He never even bothered to talk to me after our failed kiss, much less acknowledge his son to the reporter that showed up earlier this morning.

"Did you enjoy your day out?" Caleb suddenly said behind me and as I spun around I almost smashed both pizza boxes into him, but before that could happen I clutched them in my arms and crushed them against my chest. I could feel the left-over mozzarella cheese and toppings plaster against my new top.

"Oh my god, are you deliberately trying to scare me to death?" I cried out and dropped both boxes on the counter grabbing the paper towels.

Caleb didn't even flinch, he just looked at me with this dead pan expression on his face, and my insides twisted.

"I'm sorry, I thought you heard me come in," he said and tossed me a dish rag, "So did you have fun shopping?"

"It was pleasant, how was Braden," I asked quickly changing the subject.

"He was fine."

There was clearly something on Caleb's mind, he didn't quite sound like himself, and I felt an uncomfortable shiver run down my spine.

"I'm glad you spent some alone time with him," I said and turned my back on him to escape his scolding gaze.

"Why did you come here exactly?"

Well that was a little out of the blue, I'm sure I told him why I was here, "I told you why I am here, and the psychologist suggested it."

"Yeah I know what the psychologist suggested, but I want to know what *you* are doing here."

He took a step closer and I retreated, "I don't know what you're talking about, the only thing that is of any significance is getting Braden better."

"There's nothing wrong with him, he has a great imagination, and he's just misunderstood."

"What is that supposed to mean?" I blurted out, how did he dare suggest that I misunderstood my own son.

"What I meant to say is, you need to embrace all of him, that includes his other family too," he said calmly.

"Did you speak to the psychologist?" I asked fumingly.

"No, I did not, but I wasn't that much different from him, so I know exactly what he's going through. When I was a toddler I always thought I was adopted, it was like that until I was about seven years old."

That bowled me over. Caleb also had an imaginary family. Suddenly the whole concept of Lamarckism made perfect sense. I had no idea what to say to that, I simply stared at him.

"Braden needs both of us to help him through and get him to realize that we are just as important as his other family. The reason he pushes you away is because he is scared of losing his mother again,"

Caleb said and walked to the fridge to take out a bottle of water.

I never thought of it that way and the realization of what my little boy must be going through swept over me like a flood. He looked at me for a moment and then turned to leave, "Don't ever walk away from him again," and then he headed for the living room.

Chapter 11

Caleb

"I learned from the best," Rae said with such loathing, the devil himself would cringe. Instead of defending herself, she was quick to hand out punches and this game was starting to get really old.

I stopped in my tracks, turned and looked pointedly at her, "I left because it was my duty to go and defend my country, I didn't just leave because I wanted to."

I knew that was a blatant lie, I left because of my own selfish reasons, and as much as I tried to convince myself otherwise, I knew the truth.

"And I left because it was my duty to go do my hair," she bit out sarcastically.

God but she was beautiful when she was angry. Her green eyes grew a shade darker as if a storm cloud had descended overhead, and that expression alone should be terrifying, but to me it was a challenge. If I could break through that storm and survive to tell the tale I can challenge any storm that ever crossed my path.

With determination, I crossed the distance between us and cupped her face, green lightning bolts cascaded in her eyes like a thunderstorm on Jupiter. I slid one hand around the back of her neck and crushed my lips against hers. Half expecting her to shove me away, I was relieved to feel her fingers dig into my biceps as she clung to me; she wasn't fighting me this time. Her lips parted and I delved into the confines of her mouth, and her tongue met mine like a perfect dance partner. I dragged her body flush against mine and I felt her soft breasts press against my chest. My body was on fire and rigid in every sense of the word. The pent-up desire I have tried to ignore since she waltzed into my life again was reaching breaking point. I tilted her back and slid my one hand up to cup her left breast as I trailed my lips down the side of her neck to her shoulder.

"Caleb," I heard her whisper my name.

"Rae," I countered.

"Caleb," damn I loved the sound of her hushed voice and the way my name rolled off her lips.

"Caleb," she said a little louder this time and shoved lightly against me, but before I could lose all hope, she pointed at Braden.

"Damn, it's taking some time getting used to a little person in the house," I said and then grabbed her hand and led her to the nearest isolated spot in the house – the pantry.

By the time I had her cornered between the canned food and condiments she was already fumbling clumsily with the drawstring of my sweats, and I was not far behind. The simple cotton dress she wore was no deterrent for me and I quickly shoved her panties down her long legs and I lifted her up against one of the shelves.

"You know this is never going to work," she said as she wrapped her legs around my waist.

"You're right, this damn pantry is too small, but right now it will have to do," I said huskily.

I knew she wasn't referring to the confined space of the pantry, but I chose to ignore the obvious.

I spun around and knocked the potatoes off the crate that stood in the corner of the pantry and sat down with her straddling my lap and she slowly lowered herself unto my rock-hard length. And as I buried myself deep into her I felt her body tighten around me. With one hand splayed across her back, I dipped my head down and tugged on her hardened nipple through her dress.

"You feel so good," I whispered as I dragged my lips up to hers.

"Shh," she said as she held unto my shoulders and slowly started to rock her hips back and forth. Her eyes fell closed and her lips parted while the rapid bursts of her breath fanned my face. She put a spell on me, of that much I was certain, but it was one I would welcome any day. With each deliberate stroke, she bit her lip in an attempt to stifle a moan. I tried my utmost not to vocalize just how I felt this very moment, which was near impossible.

Each time her hips rose I gasped for a breath and each time they fell taking my length deep into her velvet centre I groaned. She too started panting breathlessly and the erratic movements of her hips were bringing me closer and closer to my own release. I could hardly stand it anymore, I bucked my hips upwards, rougher and harder and she met me each time. And when she bent forward and buried her face in my neck she cried out and clung to me as her body shook in my embrace. That was all I needed, every muscle in my body drew taught and with one last thrust I buried myself deep inside her, filling her with my own essence, and in the confines of the pantry it was only the two of us, and nothing else mattered.

As our frantic heart beats slowed down I held her close against me, burying my face in the crook of her neck inhaling her scent.

"This is never going to work Caleb," she said as she stood up to fix her dress.

A few days ago, that was exactly what I thought – this would never work – but now I wasn't so sure if it was just stupidity talking. I stood and pulled her into my arms and cradled her neck pressing my lips against her hair. I couldn't agree or disagree, this was already far more complex than I anticipated.

Chapter 12

Raedene

I stood in the kitchen looking out the window and watched Caleb and Braden flying a kite and my heart skipped a beat, what if this was exactly what Braden needed? He's been so caught up in this past life of his that he had missed out on being a real kid. Even though Damien tried to fill a dad's shoes in most parts of Braden's life, it was nothing like this. Braden was practically beside himself every time he got to spend time with Caleb.

Just as I turned to get back to making lunch, I spotted a suspicious character at the front gate pointing a camera at Caleb and Braden.

"Samson!" I called before storming out of the kitchen armed with a spatula.

If those reporters were back at it, I was going to give them a piece of my mind. They had no right to spy on us or take photos without our consent and I didn't give a hoot as to whether or not it was part and parcel of Caleb's claim to celebrity status. That was my son out there and I was not going to allow them to hurt him in any way.

"Samson!" I called again as I marched down the driveway towards the gate. Samson quickly fell into step beside me trying to keep up at his old age, but he too must have seen the person at the gate.

"Those vultures have no common decency; they always hover around here trying to find the next best gossip scoop for the tabloids," he said as we hurried to the gate.

The stranger saw us approaching and he hurried to take a few more shots before he scurried away. By the time we reached the gate, all we saw was a car speeding off.

"What's going on?" Caleb asked as he came to stand beside us, with Braden sitting on his hip.

"I saw a man taking photos of you," I said through gritted teeth, I knew better not to start throwing accusations around in front of Braden, "I wanted to find out what he wanted."

"I'll handle it, they come around every now and again before a big game to get an inside scoop, so I'm sure it was harmless."

"Harmless. Right," I said and stalked off towards the house.

How could he be so indifferent about this? Just the other day a reporter came asking about his son, and now this? I simply refused to expose Braden to these vultures, and if Caleb could not consider our privacy then I would have no option but to take Braden back home.

"Rae, wait!" Caleb called after me but I refused to stop.

"Rae! Hold up, can we just talk?" he said again and this time I spun around.

"Talking is just not good enough Caleb, I can't have these journalists poking around in my life, much less Braden's. Things are complicated as it is," I said folding my arms.

"I know, but unfortunately it comes with the territory, and it's not something that will just go away. They have a scoop and they will do what they can to find out what's going on, I can't change what or who I am," he said and leaned against the pillar on the wrap around veranda.

He was right, as much as I hated it; I was the one that walked into his life, not the other way around. Just because he was Braden's father didn't give me the right to make any demands. The fact remained, he was a sports star, and I was the unpopular nobody who had his child, his child. Talk about being the *insignificant* other, it was nothing short of pathetic, not to mention disastrous.

"I know, I just don't like it, and if it wasn't for that Joanne woman, they wouldn't have had a story in the first place. She feels jilted that you stood her. You should have just gone out with her. I really don't know why you bothered with me in the first place"

Caleb pushed away from the pillar and stood with his hands on his hips, "There's no proof that it was Joanne who told them anything."

"See? You even try to defend her, when the truth is staring you right in the face, unbelievable!" I spat out and then spun around and stormed into the house.

Before I knew it, Caleb had me by the arm, "I merely meant that we can't go around accusing people by mere assumption, I'll have a talk to her and find out what's going on okay?"

I tugged my arm free, "Well I'm telling you she is behind all of this, and if you think for one moment I'm going to be target practice for a scorned ex, you're wrong. Braden and I will be leaving first thing in the morning."

"No you won't," he said blankly, "Our son needs a father, and if you're too blind to see that, then you're pretty selfish. You've spent every moment of that child's life cooping him up and protecting him in this bubble of imperfection that he never had a chance to experience what it is to be a four-year-old boy!"

Blinded by rage I slapped him so hard my hand stung right into my wrist. How dare he blame me for Braden's lack of childhood experiences?

"You're a real jackass," I said furiously before I hurried up the stairs to my room. I couldn't allow him to see my tears.

Chapter 13

Caleb

I had more than enough time to think things over after our little fallout the night before, and instead of running after a raging female who could do some serious damage with that left-hand swing of hers, I left her to calm down.

In my defence I wasn't trying to protect Joanne. In fact, she was the last thing on my mind, I was just trying to contain a bad situation by playing this whole journalist thing down to me being a sports star. But if I had to be honest with myself, it was more than likely Joanne's doing and whatever her angle was for pulling such a stunt, I was not planning on letting it slide, but that was the least of my problems. I needed to reassure Rae that she belonged here and that Braden needed me.

"Has the baby sitter arrived yet?" I asked Samson as I entered the kitchen just after dawn.

"She's on her way sir," he said with a smile on his face.

"Good, when she gets here, just show her where everything is."

"Of course."

Although Samson was my butler, he was more like a father to me than my own dad had ever been and I knew that he had always liked Rae, he never made it a secret. I remember how he went out of his way to make sure he always offered Rae a ride when he picked me up from college just so that he could push us towards each other. The day I decided to leave, he was the one who told me I was making a mistake. My dad was caught up with his new girlfriend, while my mom spent days drinking herself into a stupor over his betrayal. Thinking back now, I should have listened to Samson when he told me *'she's the kind of girl who deserves more than one second chance'*. I never quite understood what he meant by that at the time, but now it was slowly starting to make sense.

Fine, so she never tried to reach me when she found out she was pregnant, but that's no reason to keep the noose around her neck. She was scared and alone, I was gone and she deserved a second chance as much as I did.

"Shall I take Miss Rae's tea up to her room?" Samson asked, drawing me out of my train of thought.

"No, I'll take it up; you tend to Maria when she arrives."

On my way to Rae's room I stopped at Braden's room, he was talking to himself again and I couldn't help but smile. He reminded me so much of myself; I had no doubt that he was going to grow up to be just fine. I could only hope that I would get to be part of it all. My heart ached just thinking of losing him.

I continued to Rae's room and knocked lightly on the door and waited, when there was no answer I entered expecting to find her sleeping, but instead I heard her in the bathroom. *Should I leave the tea and come back later or wait for her to come out of the bathroom?* I wondered. The latter option was more than just tempting and images of her wrapped only in a towel flooded my mind. I was about to leave when the door opened and as if I had telepathic powers, she exited with nothing but a towel around her.

"Oh! I-I, what are you doing here?" she asked and hugged her arms around her.

I was rendered speechless for a moment as she stood before me. Her skin was flushed and her wet hair clung to her cheeks and shoulders. As much as I wanted to take her there and then I had to control myself.

"Peace offering," I said clearing my throat. "I've brought you some tea."

"Thank you," she said and shifted her weight awkwardly; "You can just leave it on the dresser."

Pull yourself together man, I reprimanded myself and walked to the door, "Dress comfortably and meet me downstairs," I said and without waiting for her answer I left the room.

A short while later Rae came down the stairs dressed in skin tight jeans and knee high boots with a black vest that accentuated her curves. Naturally all my blood ran south and I had no choice but to force thoughts of pink bunnies and fluffy coyotes to ease the tension that rose up inside of me. If she had the slightest idea how she tempted me, she would have run away when she had the chance.

A pale young girl accompanied by Samson stepped out of the kitchen and shifted her glasses up her nose.

"Rae, this is Maria, she's going to be babysitting Braden today," I said and stepped aside.

"Hello Miss Callaway, I'm so pleased to meet you and I can assure you that Braden is in great hands," Maria said reassuringly.

Rae's jaw dropped as she looked at Maria, then at me, and back at Maria, "I'm sorry Maria, I think there was a slight misunderstanding, we won't need your services."

"Of course we do." I placed my hand on Rae's shoulder and forced a smile.

"No we don't," she bit out and shrugged away from me.

"Just work with me here, okay?" I turned and looked at Maria, "Can you give us a moment?

"Of course, I'll go tend to Braden."

"Why the hell would you make these decisions without consulting me?" Rae said the moment Maria was out of sight.

"I've arranged a baby sitter so that I can take you out for a bit, you need it," I took her by the shoulders and looked into her eyes.

"She's a complete stranger and I don't need to go out, I just need to be with Braden."

"She has good references, the agency reassured me she can be trusted and Samson is also here to keep an eye on everything."

Rae turned out of my grasp and walked to the doorway then spun around and whispered under her breath, "How do you know she's not an undercover journalist?"

I threw my head back and laughed shaking my head, "You watch far too many CSI episodes, she's not a journalist, she is only sixteen and trying to save for college. I promise you she will not jeopardize her income. My managers' wife runs an Au Pair company and she owed me a favour, Maria is one of the best on her payroll and she can be trusted."

She scrunched her nose up and then bit her thumb, "I just don't think it's wise to leave him with a complete stranger, you know how he gets."

I looked over her shoulder at Maria sitting with Braden on the floor. Braden was a little tentative and had distanced himself from Maria, but he was also not shying away from her completely. In fact, he had shoved some of his Legos over to her.

"Rae, he's a little boy with a great imagination, he'll be safe and sound here with Maria and Samson and I think the more he is exposed to other people the better it is for him."

"What, so now you're a specialist in the field of what he needs, while you weren't around half of his life?" she bit out and the moment she did her hand flew to her mouth and I knew she did not mean to say what she said.

I clenched my jaw and pinched the bridge of my nose. Now was not the time to throw stones and instead of reacting to her allegations, I reached for the helmet on the table and held it out to her along with a leather jacket that conveniently popped up out of no-where. I could only guess it was one of the cheer leaders' jackets that got abandoned after one of the many parties I've hosted at my house, but Rae didn't have to know that.

"I'm not taking no for an answer," I simply stated and then walked out the door.

Part of me expected the helmet to fly out the door and hit me against the back of my head, but it never did. Instead Rae stepped out of the house dressed in the leather jacket with the helmet in her hand.

"Caleb, I'm sorry," she said as she shuffled closer, "that was uncalled for, it's just that I have never left Braden on his own with a complete stranger, and I get nervous."

I got that she was trying to protect him, but I also knew she was going about it the wrong way, "I know you are worried, I just think it's time you give him a chance to spread his wings," I reached up to trace a single finger along the angular line of her jaw, "When it comes to raising kids, I'm the last one to give advice, but I know myself and I promise you if I had a mother that cooped me up like a porcelain doll, I would also pretend I had another family."

That made her laugh, "I'm not that bad."

"Wanna bet?" I grinned and tugged her earlobe playfully and the way her eyes fluttered closed as she inclined her head into my touch nearly made me change my mind and take her back inside and to my bed instead, she was simply irresistible.

Chapter 14

Raedene

The moment we hit the open road and Caleb opened the throttle I felt the adrenalin rush through me and the tension from moments earlier eased away. He was right, I have been cooping Braden up far too much, but in my defence all mothers tend to do that with the first born, or so I read. I forced my insecurities about the baby sitter and leaving Braden with a stranger aside, and decided to just enjoy the moment.

Being on the back of a bike with my chest pressed against Caleb's back brought back memories. When we were younger he always used to give me a ride on his bike whenever he rode it, we were wild and free back then. The golden couple that everyone always thought would end up together.

The day was perfect, the wind was cool but not cold, and the leather jacket he gave me was enough to shield me from the cool breeze as it whipped past us. We rode for what seemed like a few minutes when Caleb took a left into Denver itself. I couldn't help but contain my own excitement not knowing what he had planned. It felt like Deja vu, the scents and smells that filled my senses reminded me of so many things, things I had forgotten over the years, and now being here with him, the memories all started flooding back.

We finally pulled up outside a steakhouse called Mickey's. Caleb got off the bike and then helped me to take the helmet off.

"I see your hair didn't suffer any damage," he said smiling.

I laughed and shook my hair, "Cocooned like that, I highly doubt a typhoon would touch my hair."

He chuckled, and handed me my helmet "Hang on to yours, you hungry?"

I took a deep breath and as the smell of food assaulted my senses, my stomach rumbled, "Does that answer your question?"

"Sure does."

He laced his fingers with mine and led me to the entrance, other than the waiters and the odd patron the place was empty. I glanced around at the interior; it was a homely place that indicated the owner insisted on a personal touch. On the far wall, next to the bar was a bunch of framed photographs, all sports related and among them, rugby photos. I spotted one in particular. It was Caleb flying through the air with arms stretched out and a ball in his hands.

"Is that you scoring a tri?" I asked curiously.

"Yes ma'am, that's our golden boy," it was an elderly man who spoke next to me, "Caleb here is a real sports hero; he makes us proud every time he gets on the field."

"Morgan buddy," Caleb said and let go of my hand, then clasped hands with Morgan and bumped shoulders, "You shouldn't be exaggerating like that, it's a team sport."

"Oh that's no exaggeration, that tri won us the game, and so did many others," Morgan said.

I felt like the odd one out between the two men as they chatted about ruby, it was as if I didn't exist. I slid away awkwardly to look at the other pictures that lined the walls leaving the two of them to catch up. I couldn't believe how I never noticed that Caleb was famous, he was really a celebrity in these parts and probably the country and there I was, completely oblivious to what was going on in the world of sports. I used to be a fan when I was in college but only because I was trying to impress him, but after that I hardly watched sports, much less read the sports section in the newspapers. I blamed Damien too, if he knew all along that Caleb was Braden's father he should have kept me in the loop, surely he knew all along where Caleb found himself and how popular he had become.

"Miss Callaway?" A young man spoke next to me.

"Yes?" I turned to look at him.

"My name is Justin, I'm from the Daily News, and I was wondering if you would mind answering a few questions?"

"Listen here..." I started but before I could finish my sentence, Morgan had the man by the scruff dragging him to the door.

"They just won't let it go," Caleb said as he came to stand next to me, "I'm sorry Rae."

"It's okay, I suppose it comes with the territory," I looked towards the door where Morgan still stood with his arms crossed over his chest, "Looks like you have your personal body guard at least."

"Ah, this is the only place I can eat in peace without reporters harassing me." He slid his hand under my elbow and led me to one of the tables in the far corner away from the window.

"It's a nice place, very cosy."

"It is, Morgan prides himself in making sure this place stays a family establishment where everyone can have a decent meal away from home."

"A family restaurant, so why do you come here?" the words slipped out before I could stop them, but Caleb just smiled.

"Great food, it beats the best steakhouses in town."

"Fair enough."

I slipped into the seat opposite Caleb and glanced at the menu, printed on the placemat.

"It's still early, so if you want something light I won't hold it against you, but I'm starving," he said grinning.

"It's just after ten in the morning, so I'll stick to a breakfast," I said pointing to the Country Breakfast. "Eggs, bacon and toast with a side of fries, that's all I will be able to eat."

Caleb opted for a rump steak and by the time the waitress took our order Morgan had already sent some coffee over.

I kept looking towards the door, nervous that another reporter might try and sneak in, but Caleb didn't seem too deterred.

"So, when last have you been out and about to have some fun?"

"Plenty," I lied.

"Come on Rae, you're lying to me."

"No I'm not," I smiled and tore of the tip of the sugar sachet and poured the sugar into my coffee, "I'm not a recluse, I just don't- I don't spend my nights partying anymore."

"I wasn't talking about partying; I was talking about dating or just hanging out with friends. Surely you have dated since Braden was born?"

Caleb was fishing for information, trying to stir the water and see what secrets lay below the surface.

"I tried once, it was a complete failure. He turned out to be gay."

"He was gay?" Caleb said laughing, "You must have been one hell of a date to send him running in the other direction."

I reached over the table and slapped his shoulder, "That was not my doing. He was a closet case, didn't want anyone to know and I was his alibi."

"So what happened?"

"Well," I giggled, "We went ice skating one night, and he had disappeared at some point in the evening so I went looking for him. Let's just say, I found him in a very compromising position with another guy and that was the end of it."

Caleb roared with laughter and sat back crossing his arms over his chest, "I would have loved to be a fly on the wall."

"How about you?" I asked tentatively, "How many women have you dated?"

He shifted in his chair and looked everywhere accept at me.

"Come on, I told you about my experience, now it's your turn."

"I won't say I've dated anyone steadily for some time, being on the team, I'm always busy at practice or playing the game."

"Liar, what about Joanne, she seemed like she had a different idea."

He scratched his head and then dragged his hand down the back of his neck, "She's one of the cheer leaders, and they are all like rabid dogs trying to get their teeth into us. It's quite shocking, but convenient if you want no strings attached."

"Woah, referring to women as dogs is derogatory. That's not nice," I laughed.

"You know what I mean; to them it's all about fame, which player they are latched on to and how much publicity they get being on a sports star's arm."

"So you never went on dates, dinner, dance, sex?"

Oh my god, I did not just ask him the sex question, that was a little too direct but it literally slipped out.

"Dinner yes, dance no, sex yes," he said as he tapped his fingers on the table, "I'm a hot-blooded male; sex is something that comes naturally."

I felt my cheeks grow hot and I averted my eyes, "That's true I suppose."

Caleb's hand cupped mine unexpectedly and I looked up to meet his eyes.

"Sex is not making love, there is a distinct difference," he said as if to justify his response.

"It's in the same category as the birds and the bees lesson Caleb," I joked and tried to pull my hand free but he held on.

"It is but it's different, men are animals, I'm not going to beat around the bush with you. We only have enough blood to operate one head at a time, and sometimes it's not even enough to feed our hearts."

I rolled my eyes and forced a smile, "Why are you trying to defend yourself? It's not as if I was going to hold it against you, it's been over five years and what you did with your free time has nothing to do with me."

Caleb let go of my hand and sat back as the waitress came with our orders. Suddenly I didn't feel as hungry as I did earlier, in fact the hollow feeling of regret that filled my insides was enough to keep me away from food for the rest of the day.

"I regret leaving you," he said once the waitress was gone.

"Well shit happens, and you had a lot going on."

"Rae, look at me," he said and reached for both my hands stilling them, "I was confused, I'm not going to lie, and I was angry, but I should never have taken it out on you."

I smiled at him then, "Are you here to have breakfast or seek absolution for your sins? It was a long time ago and we both moved on with life."

He looked at me with an intensity that took my breath away, and before I could say a word he pushed himself up and reached over the table sliding his hand behind my head, then crushed his lips against mine. I could taste the coffee on his tongue and his scent flooded my nostrils and I was lost, his kiss suddenly felt like a whispered promise, one I wanted to believe with all my heart.

When he finally pulled away, he looked deeply into my eyes and it was as if everything around us had faded to black.

"It was always you," he said and then slowly sat back down and casually took a sip of his coffee.

We ate our food in silence but there was no denying the sexual tension that was building between us. My mind was a muddled mess and all I could think of was how intense that kiss was. It was as if it drilled down into my soul to arrest my heart.

Chapter 15

Caleb

That kiss was the defining moment when I realized that I was still very much in love with Rae. Regardless of the past, and how my own parents' marriage ruined my outlook on the happily-ever-after aspect. No two people could be more entwined than us at this very point in time. We spent the rest of the morning walking the streets of Denver enjoying each other's company, I kept checking with Samson to make sure Braden was fine just so I could put Rae's mind at ease. After sightseeing, I had one more stop to make before we headed home.

"Can you bear to be in my company a little while longer?"

"Depends on what it all entails," Rae said and put the helmet on.

"You will like it, I promise."

"We'll see."

I revved the engine and set off, I liked how Rae's arms felt around me when she clung to me and I was tempted to speed up a bit, but then the thought did cross my mind that she might squeeze the air from my lungs and we'll end up in the nearest ditch.

A few minutes later I pulled into the parking lot of the Botanical Gardens and again helped Rae off the bike. This time we left the helmets on the bike and made our way through the large gates. It was late noon and the sun had already started to set, there were only a few other couples around, so I picked one of the benches near the willow trees and water pond that looked like a deck of lilies. With the sun already disappearing, so did the star white flowers, but the fragrance still hung heavily in the air.

"This place is breath taking," Rae said as she sat down on the bench.

"It really is, I don't think it gets nearly enough credit, the locals don't always appreciate the beauty of this place."

"Wasn't this where one of those corpse flowers bloomed recently?" she asked curiously.

I was impressed, very few people were aware of the sudden anomaly that hit the US by storm after multiple corpse flowers bloomed around the same time, "Yeah it's in one of the pavilions, but it's not blooming anymore. I was on tour when it happened otherwise I would have been here to watch it bloom."

"I would have loved to see it, better luck next time," she said smiling.

"I'll make sure you see the next bloom."

She was sitting up with her back straight and her hands planted on her knees. From her casual demeanour earlier, she almost came across as nervous now.

"Are you okay?"

"Of course I am, why do you ask?"

"You just seem, I don't know, tense."

"I just, I've never been away from Braden this long, and its already starting to get dark."

I moved closer to her and wrapped my arm around her shoulders, then took her hand in mine and pressed my lips against her finger tips, "Braden is fine, I've been checking with Samson every hour."

She sighed, "I know, I'm being silly."

At that opportune moment, the entire place lit up in a display of beautiful colours that transformed the gardens into something more like a magical fairy garden, and that was all it took to draw Rae's attention.

"Oh my god, this is absolutely breath taking," she stood up and turned around, "I've never seen anything like it."

I smiled and came to stand next to her near the pond, "They do this every evening, it's like a tradition, it's even more beautiful in winter, and then it's more like Whoville at Christmas."

Rae suddenly giggled and I couldn't help but laugh, "You remember when we watched the Grinch? That movie was sooo funny, I want Braden to watch it this Christmas."

I chuckled, "We will have to make sure he watches *Horton Hears a Who* first, he's going to need to know where the Who's come from."

Yep, I just said 'we', and by the way Rae's mouth fell open and her eyes met mine, I knew that she read between the lines, and suddenly there it was, that sexual tension I have been trying to ignore since the kiss at Mickey's, but now here in this magical place the lights and all the colours served as the fireworks one can expect when you look at a beautiful woman and realize she's feeling exactly the same.

I stepped in, and so did she; my heart thumped with hope at her approach. I wrapped my arms around her waist and she gripped the front of my shirt and our lips met midway. Her breath mixed with mine and filled my lungs and I let out an audible groan, how I wish we were completely alone. I slid my hands down and pulled her more firmly against me, wanting not to scare her, but show her exactly what she did to me. Instead of pulling away she leaned harder against me. As she slid one hand up and around my neck her other hand found the hem of my shirt and slipped under it. The moment her cool fingers touched my skin, I knew I was damned.

"Rae..." I whispered as I pulled away from the kiss, cupping her face, "Baby if we don't stop now, the trees and the flowers are going to have a lot more to talk about than bees."

She tucked her teeth into her bottom lip and smiled mischievously up at me, then slid her hand further under my shirt until she cupped my left peck, "Then I suggest you take me home right this minute, or we'll put nature to shame."

I gritted my teeth as I felt her hand slide from my chest to my stomach to stop just above my jeans, she had the art of seduction down to perfection and anything she did from this moment on would put me at risk of breaking the law and being locked up for indecent exposure. Determined I took her hand and lead her back out of the gardens to the motorbike.

"Get on, before I go insane," I said and she laughed.

"Yes sir!"

Chapter 16

Raedene

By the time we got home my body was on fire, sitting pressed up against Caleb's back was excruciating, all I could think of was his lips on mine and those intense eyes that that bore into my soul. The moment he turned the bike of I scrambled off and rushed into the house and I knew he was short on my heels, but I had to check on Braden first.

"Samson, Maria?" I whispered as I entered the living room.

"Hi," Maria said as she excited the kitchen, "Braden's asleep upstairs, he went to bed about an hour ago."

"He never goes to bed so early," I said concerned.

"Well we had a lot of fun and he was so exhausted. He did have something to eat before he passed out, so don't worry."

"Oh okay then, I'll go look in on him," I walked to the stairs then turned, "Maria. Thank you."

"No problem."

I ran up the stairs and quietly opened Braden's door. He was fast asleep hugging a plush toy bear to his chest. My heart ached as I looked down at him sleeping and I brushed a lock of hair from his brow.

"Sweet dreams my boy," I whispered and then kissed his forehead before I quietly left his room.

As I entered the hallway, Caleb was there waiting for me and from the way he looked at me, I knew he was also reaching the end of his sanity. Without a word, I grabbed his hand and pulled him into my bedroom.

The moment the door closed, Caleb spun me around and pressed me up against the door. He lowered his one hand to my hip and his fingers brushed the bare skin between my vest and jeans, which sent a shiver of pleasure coursing through me. I sighed as his lips met mine and I knew that there was no turning back now. I slid my hands down to his waist and pulled him tighter against me and that was encouragement enough. In one swift motion, he reached for my vest and pulled it off over my head and his hands instantly cupped my breasts, and even though they were covered in lace I could feel the heat of his palms burn into my skin. I followed suit and pulled his T-shirt off and the sight of him took my breath away. He was all muscle and ripped abs and I knew that it could make any woman swoon helplessly at his feet. I felt a stab of jealousy poke at my subconscious knowing that other women had seen him like this, but the moment his hands moved to the buttons of my jeans those thoughts fled for the hills.

We undressed each other eagerly until we stood naked in front of each other.

"You are so beautiful," he whispered as he drew me into his arms.

"You're biased," I joked as I ran my fingers down his chest stopping just above the V that cut down in front of his stomach. I felt his stomach muscles contract and tighten and I smiled.

"I promise you that this has nothing to do with being biased, it's the honest truth," he groaned and lifted me effortlessly into his arms then carried me over to the bed.

I met his eyes and his desire reflected my own, I needed him, I needed to feel him make love to me, but before I would allow myself that pleasure, I wanted him to know exactly how much I needed him. As he stood at the edge of the bed, I sat up and looked at him with a smile tugging at my lips while I ran my hands up along his thighs to his waist. He was rock hard and as I reached to wrap my hand around his erection, he cursed under his breath.

"Too much, too soon?" I asked smiling as I stroked him.

"Hell no, but if you keep that up, it will be the quickest climax in history," he said in a strained tone.

"I doubt that very much."

I lowered my head and took him into my mouth, his hands fisted my hair as I rolled my tongue around his tip as his hips started to move. With my one hand at his base, I dragged my tongue along his full length and then sucked him into my mouth again.

"Oh my god Rae..." he uttered breathlessly.

"Not even god can save you now," I said and continued teasing him.

As I pleasured him with my mouth he groaned audibly and rocked his hips, not once letting go of my hair. I could feel my own arousal as the wetness between my legs increased. I was lost in time and space and the present was all that mattered. Before I knew it, Caleb had tugged me away from him and was now laying on top of me, kissing me with such passion I thought I was going to faint. I felt his hand slide down over my stomach and between my legs and when his fingers slid between my folds I cried out, "Caleb, please!" I was slowly coming undone.

"Patience," he said and I could feel him smile against my skin as he pressed kisses along my jaw, down my throat and between my breasts. He moved his lips to one of my nipples and sucked the aching tip into his mouth. It was like a magical chord of ecstasy that connected every nerve ending in my body to each other. And while he slid his fingers in and out of my wetness and sucked on my nipple I felt my entire world spiral out of control.

He moved up along my body again until our eyes met and as he lay nestled between my thighs I raised my knees, spreading myself for him.

"Are you sure about this," he asked with a smile tugging on his lips.

"Is the pope catholic?" I asked dragging my nails up along his spine.

"His loyalty is questionable," he joked and then slid his rock-hard length between my slick folds.

"Oh god, just..." I started, unable to formulate a coherent sentence.

"Say please," he teased.

"You're making me beg?"

"Maybe."

"Seriously?"

Caleb looked down at me and I bit my bottom lip and in one smooth motion he moved his hips and entered me slowly at first, but with each stroke he became more relentless, thrusting faster and harder. I wrapped my legs around his thighs and gripped his biceps as he thrusted, over and over. I arched my back and met his every stroke; overwhelmed by the intensity of the moment I could feel every nerve ending in my body tingle and rise to the pinnacle of pleasure.

"Caleb," I uttered over and over as I felt my body and mind slipping further and further into oblivion. Each thrust of his cock into my core drove me closer and closer to the edge and I knew that he too, was reaching that tipping point. When he called out my name my entire world came undone and I surrendered myself completely to him.

For a while after, I lay cradled in his arms while he drew patterns over my back and arms, something I always loved. Everything felt perfect, it was as if our stars were aligned and nothing and no one could ruin this sacred moment.

"When you said that *we* have to show Braden *Horton hears a who*, did you just say that?"

I felt the smile tug at his lips and then he pressed his lips against the top of my head.

"I meant it; Braden deserves to have us both in his life."

I closed my eyes and bit my lip, for now I'll take what I can get and leave the empty promises and unhappily ever after's, for when they rear their ugly heads.

Chapter 17

Caleb

I looked down at the financials, it's the first time in weeks since I've visited the office and I knew I had to show face sooner or later. It was fun having a board of members running the show, but in reality, I couldn't keep hiding from obvious obligations.

"Mr. Hayes, your manager is here to see you," my secretary announced.

"Send him in."

"Gary, this is a pleasant surprise, didn't expect to see you here," I said and sat down, "surely you could have caught up with me at practice tomorrow."

"Unfortunately, this cannot wait Caleb. There are stories flying around left right and centre and it's not helping your image."

"What stories?"

"Well some reckon the girl is leading you on and that she's just a gold digger after your money," he said and shifted uncomfortably.

"And who may I ask would be spreading these rumours?"

"Everyone, we've had reporters peeping around at the club and asking questions. They want to know if you did a paternity test to prove that the child is yours."

"Is that so?"

Grant stood up and walked over to the window, "I know it's not my place, but maybe you should insist on a paternity test. Some women will go to any length to get what they want."

Not Rae, I thought as I collected the papers and placed them into a manila folder, but if that is what the public wants I don't see why it will be a bad thing. I knew for a fact Braden was my son, and I was more than certain that Rae was no gold digger.

"I'll arrange a paternity test, but then I want you to handle the journalists," I said and as I looked up I saw Rae standing at the door, her face as white a sheet.

"Rae," I said and stood up, but the look on her face told me to stay put.

"A paternity test, so that's what you plan to do?" she bit out coldly, "Don't bother Caleb, I'll be gone before you get home." And without a word she spun around and walked away.

"For god sakes," I cursed and ran off after her, "Rae, wait!"

She spun around and shoved her finger against my chest, "No! I'm done Caleb. Braden is much better and we do not need you or your money. I can do this on my own, I don't need you."

I dragged my hands through my hair and sighed frustratingly. Going after her now would simply provoke her, I had to give her some time to calm down and then talk to her. So, I watched her leave and I cursed under my breath.

"She's up to something, Caleb, otherwise she would have agreed to a paternity test. What has she got to hide?"

I strode towards Grant and grabbed him by his shirt, I was fuming, I had enough of managers trying to rule my every decision and journalists hounding me down, "She is not hiding anything!" I said angrily before shoving him away from me, "Braden is my son, and I don't give a shit what everyone else believes. You do what you're supposed to do and handle it, it's what you get paid for."

Grant stumbled back and then fixed his shirt and headed for the door, "This will leave a mark on your career."

"Then maybe you should start looking a replacement."

I looked at the time and although I desperately wanted to get home to Rae to sort this mess out, I had to attend the general board meeting first. I cursed under my breath and then marched to the boardroom.

Chapter 18

Raedene

A week later I sat in my own apartment back home in Lafayette, and every day there was a few more missed calls from Caleb, which I refused to answer. The fact that he even suggested a paternity test was enough for me to make up my mind. To find out that he had the slightest doubt about Braden hurt more than anything and I simply refused to stay under the same roof as him.

I paged aimlessly through a magazine trying to keep my mind off Caleb, but in all honestly reading a local sports magazine wasn't the best therapy either. On every second page, there was mention of the famous Caleb Hayes, or the Denver Stampede and although I didn't exactly read the articles his name jumped out at me like a bad memory.

"Mommy," Braden called out as he came running into the room, "look what I made."

My heart stopped and I dropped the magazine. Did he just call me mommy? I was beside myself, he has never referred to me as his mom, but I knew I couldn't exactly make a fuss about it, so I forced my own excitement aside and looked at him, "Let's see what you have there."

It was a picture with a house and a family; this time instead of his other family, he had drawn three people and I knew exactly who the third person was. A lump formed in my throat and I fought back the tears. What on earth was I going to do?

"Wow, this is beautiful, is that Uncle Caleb?" I asked and cleared my throat.

"Yep, he's my new daddy, I want to visit him."

I let out a controlled breath and hugged my little boy. Decision made, I had to move to Denver so that Braden could see Caleb whenever he wanted, but that would mean I would have to agree to a paternity test. Maybe it wasn't such a bad idea, but I don't think I would be able to put my heart on the line again. I was sure that I could live in the same town as

Caleb without melting into a puddle of goo every time he looked at me.

"I'm sure he would like that," I said and then lifted him unto my lap, "Caleb is playing Rugby now, do you want to watch the game with me?"

"He's on the TV?"

"Yes he is," I said and flicked to the sports channel.

We sat and watched the game and at half time I made us a quick snack. Initially the sport did not interest me, but seeing the players on the field and how excited Braden got each time he saw Caleb had me hooked. Half time was over and the players all jogged back onto the field and the game got underway. The Denver Stampede was leading 18 – 6, but the players looked exhausted from their efforts. Each bone crunching tackle had me on edge; I've never been one for such barbaric sports, and watching players being carried off on stretchers or with cuts in their faces made me nervous.

Ten minutes into half time, Caleb was sprinting to the try line, one of the opposition players came storming him from the side and when he collided with Caleb, he was catapulted into the air and came down head first and that's where he stayed. I looked at Braden and was grateful that he was busy playing with his Legos instead of watching the game. I glanced back at the screen; the referee had blown the whistle and raised his arms above his head with his wrists crossed. Within seconds, paramedics came rushing unto the field with a spine board and I held my breath for a second and when the live broadcast was interrupted, I knew something went horribly wrong.

***

Hours later I sat next to Caleb where he lay in traction. He had suffered a compression fracture on his C5-C6 vertebrae which caused pressure on his spinal cord, leaving him paralysed. And although the doctor reassured me that it was only temporary, I couldn't help but worry.

In his sedated state, I took his hand in mine, "I know you can't hear me, but I'm going to say this anyway. You have to get better, Braden needs you and-and I need you."

Realisation swept over me as I rubbed my thumb over the back of his hand. I still loved him after all these years and coming so close to losing him after just finding him scared me more than anything. Outside reporters gathered to get a scoop of the story but Samson was determined to not allow anyone in, which I was thankful for.

"Rae..."

Caleb was waking up and even though he couldn't move, a smile tugged at his lips.

"Caleb, you stupid fool," I said and shifted closer to him, "You scared the hell out of me. How are you feeling?"

"Right now I'm not feeling much at all," he said and I could see the laughter in his eyes. Unbelievable! Even at this point he could make silly jokes.

"It's not funny, you could have broken your neck," I said and squeezed his hand.

"It will be convenient though, you would have to look after me for life then," he said in his croaky voice.

His response caught me off guard and I could only smile, "I'm serious Caleb, what would I have told Braden?"

The door to the room opened unexpectedly and I turned to see who entered expecting Samson, but instead it was two men I haven't seen before.

"Mr. Hayes, I'm from the Daily Tribune..." one of them started and I instantly got my back up and glared at them.

"Have you no consideration, you can see he's not well, get out of here this instant!" I ground out and went to stand between Caleb and the parasites.

"Are you Miss Callaway, the mother of his child?"

God, he was relentless. I was about to attack him physically when Caleb spoke up.

"It's okay Rae, I can handle this," he said.

I hesitated and then stepped aside.

Caleb looked at me and then at the reporter, "For the record, Miss Rae Callaway is the mother of my child, and no, I'm not going to fight for custody. I plan on marrying her," he said and then glanced my way.

I was too overwhelmed to say anything; my mouth fell open and closed a few times.

"That is if she will have me," he continued while the reporter's camera man clicked away taking photos.

I glanced at Caleb and caught him watching me. What just happened? He just stated to the reporter that he wanted to marry me. I was sure it was his concussion speaking, so I moved closer and leaned down to whisper, "You don't have to pretend for the press, they can make their own conclusions, I don't really care, I just want you to get better."

"I'm not pretending, it's the truth, I am in love with you."

Shocked I sat down not trusting my own legs, even the reporter and camera man stood silently watching. I knew I had to say something but words failed me, so instead I leaned over and pressed my lips against his.

"Is that a yes or a maybe?" he asked against my lips.

"It's a maybe, first get better so that you can get on your knees to propose," I whispered and then kissed him, the other people in the room forgotten.

Epilogue

Two months later Braden and I went with Samson to meet Caleb at his physiotherapist. He had been working hard to get back on his feet, and was finally able to take more than twenty steps before having to rest. When I entered the rehabilitation centre it was decorated with gold balloons and white roses all over the place. At the far end, I spotted Damien and his fiancée standing among the staff along with a bunch of really big bulky men who I could only assume were Celeb's rugby mates. Caleb stood near the parallel walking bar in a suit. I glanced around the room and slowly approached him with Braden holding my hand.

Caleb looked at me and smiled and with the help of his physiotherapist he went down on one knee and held out a little velvet box.

"Rae Callaway, I'm on my knees finally, so will you do me the honour of being my partner in crime?" he said with a grin. Around us everyone stood holding their breaths and waiting in anticipation, some of the women were dabbing tears from their eyes and I was pretty close to tears myself.

I looked down at Braden and then asked him, "So do you want Caleb to be your real dad?"

Braden didn't even wait; he launched at Caleb and hugged him tightly. I smiled and went down on my knees then leaned in and kissed him, "I would want nothing more," I said softly and Caleb slid the ring unto my trembling finger.

Finally, my life was starting to get direction, my son finally accepted me as his only mother, while I had the love of my life right by my side, nothing could be more prefect that this.

*****

THE END

Excerpt of Her Fake Fiancé Billionaire Boss

Everything would be fine. At the worst, she would laugh and think he was pulling her leg or at best she would take the offer without another question.

Justin Dunne's workday was coming to an end. At any minute his assistant Jennifer would come by to tell him that she was leaving. When she came in he would ask her the thing he had been trying to think of a way to properly phrase all day. He felt small in his large office dreading what he was about to do. What was the worst that could happen? If she said no she would just leave and then come back to work the next day like nothing happened. Could this count as sexual harassment? He sat at his desk and ran his fingers through his hair a couple times. Everything would be fine, he told himself hearing the soft knock at the door.

He looked up hearing Jennifer walking into his office. She had her purse with her and had a coat on, signaling she was ready to head out. He smiled and stood up.

"Jennifer," he said.

"Mr. Dunne, I just came to say I'll be heading out. Was there anything you wanted me to do before I did?"

"Just one thing Jennifer, please sit." He motioned to the chair directly across from his at his large, glass-top desk. Jennifer looked at him quizzically, heading for the seat.

"Is there something wrong?"

He walked past her, heading to the bar which he kept stocked with drinks. If he wanted to he could live in his office and not have any reason to leave. He had a closet full of clean work clothes, a bathroom, a bar and a phone call could have any meal of his choice brought to him at his desk.

"Drink?" he asked. The bar was near the wall. It was less a wall and more a floor to ceiling window that gave him a dizzying view of the city when he looked out of it; just one of the perks of working on the top floor. The view was breathtaking but the vertigo-inducing height didn't help his trepidation right then.

"No, I'm fine. What is this about sir?" she asked again. Jennifer sat at the desk watching her boss's back as he poured himself a drink. The last time she had sat in that seat was when she was being interviewed for the job. Mr. Dunne's jacket, vest and tie had been abandoned sometime before she had come in and he had rolled his sleeves up. He had thick, sinewy forearms which were certainly not built from hours typing at a computer. Slight worry ran through her wondering what it was that he wanted to talk to her about. She knew she wasn't in trouble, or at least she hoped she wasn't.

He regarded her as she sat. Her legs were crossed making the skirt she was wearing ride up slightly, not enough to be inappropriate but enough to catch his attention. He was professional but he was not blind. Jennifer's hair was a rich chestnut tone, with lighter brown highlights throughout. She was probably something close to average height because she was still quite a bit shorter than he was in her heels. A past of swimming through high school and college had given her an athletic form, accented by a generous chest that her conservative work blouses did not hide.

"I have something to ask you Jennifer." He stayed standing, walking slowly by her as he rounded the desk. "You know about the deal with Pryor?"

"He's the one you want to buy the property from in Midtown," she said.

"That's right. He's shown additional interest in becoming an investor with us."

"That's fantastic," she said, not knowing what else to say. She wondered what that had to do with her. She wasn't Pryor's assistant, she was his. If he wanted a scheduled meeting with Pryor or whatever else, he could have easily told her over the phone after she had left, or just opened with it instead of making a speech. It wasn't that she didn't take her work seriously but she wanted to leave. Her workday was over and she couldn't wait to go home and take her heels off.

"It is. I'm having him over to my house for dinner to discuss the deal," he said, swirling the liquid around his glass.

"Do you want me to schedule it? Get in contact with him? Send a car over?"

"No. You see Jennifer... I've been thinking all day about how to ask you this. There is no easy way to say it."

"What is it?"

"I told Mr. Pryor that I would receive him Friday night at my home... with my fiancée."

They looked at each other for a few silent moments. "Do you want me to send her a car?"

"That would be difficult, seeing as I am not engaged to be married," he said.

"Then who is hosting the dinner with you? You want me to call him and say it will just be you two?"

"I was hoping that you wouldn't have to. What I want Jennifer, is for you to host the dinner with me." Jennifer was silent for a second, searching his face for any mirth. There was none. If anything, his face was cold and serious. His blue eyes betrayed worry and anxiety. Jennifer panicked suddenly realizing he was serious. His usually impeccably styled black hair was tousled like he'd been running his hands through it.

"What?"

"I want to introduce you as my fiancée to Pryor."

Here is a FREE SPECIAL BONUS BOOK

Traded to the Mob

Chapter 1

Louis lazily leaned against the door jamb as the tall promiscuous blonde left with her shoes in her hand. She was just one of many who passed through this door in the past few months.

"Louis," his father said tautly, "you need a wife."

"*Scusami*?" he asked and turned to his father, "you can't be serious."

"I am dead serious. I will not allow you to bring these whores into my home. These debauched ways of yours is bringing shame to our family name."

"It's the twenty first century, and it's called entertainment. I have no need or desire to find myself bound to one woman for the rest of my life," Louis stated and closed the front door.

"This is not a request, and if you do not find a wife, I will find one for you," his father stated matter-of-factly.

Unbelievable, if it wasn't enough that his father called the shots for everything related to the family business. He was now calling the shots on his life. But he knew better than to go against his father's wishes. Stefano Angelino was one of the most feared Dons in Italian circles and he did not make idle threats. When he gave an order, everyone jumped, and if they didn't, they simply disappeared. And being his father's right hand man and advisor didn't exclude him from this harsh reality.

He threw his hands in the air and shook his head, "*Bene*! I'll find a wife if that pleases you," he exclaimed.

There was a calculated silence as Stefano stood studying his son's reaction. He may be considered an old fool where his children were concerned but he wasn't born yesterday. He knew when he was being played, and right now Louis was simply in agreement for the sake of it. If he had to leave it up to his son to pick his own wife, who knows what wet rat he'll drag into this house. With money at his every beck and call he could pay a woman to pretend to be his wife.

"I will pick your wife for you," he said determined and by the look on Louis' face, the curveball undeniably caught his son off guard.

"Is forcing me to marry not enough, now you wish to pick my bride?" Louis rambled off angrily. "If mother was alive she would not have allowed this at all."

"You will have respect for the dead Louis," he said and glared at his son, "Gino Benedetti and his family will be visiting us from America and you will ask for his daughter's hand in marriage, *capisci*?"

He could see the cogs turning in his son's head. The moment when it dawned on Louis that having Gino's daughter as his daughter-in-law presented the opportunity to have a greater foothold in New York was perfect.

"You are marrying me off to Belinda? She's a terrible match father; she's a shy faded grey mouse."

Stefano laughed and shook his head, "You haven't seen her in almost ten years. How can you know what she is like now? You'll ask for her hand in marriage, and that's the end of it."

Louis stared after his father in disbelief, this cannot possibly be happening? Belinda of all people is to become his wife. He walked over to the drinks cabinet and poured himself a whiskey, his brain kicking into gear. *I will ask for her hand in marriage father, but you can only lead a horse to the water,* he thought wickedly and tossed the amber liquid down his throat.

Chapter 2

Belinda tuned out her friend Natalie's constant nagging about weight loss, *Banting* this, and *Banting* that, she was Italian for god sakes and had no time for fad diets. Italians lived to eat, it was their culture, hence the fact that she loved her job as the head chef and manageress at her father's restaurant. She may have spent all her teenage years in New York, but she still kept her Italian heritage. She looked at the stock list again and then handed it to her friend.

"This should be enough to last you for the next two weeks. And before you know it, I'll be back," she said sounding almost too positive. She hated having to leave the restaurant in someone else's care. Even if Natalie was her most trusted friend and the best sous chef she ever had the pleasure to work with, she hated shifting her responsibilities unto others.

"I'll be fine Bee, I promise and so will the restaurant. You won't have a thing to worry about," her friend reassured her.

"I know. It's just that two weeks is such a long time to be away from El Pescore. I still think I can convince my father to let me stay behind," she said tapping her index finger on her lips.

"You haven't had a vacation in over three years, and you love Italy, so now is your chance. Just go and come back in one piece," Natalie said and tugged the stock list out of Belinda's hand. "And if you happen to find a hot Italian hunk, get his number."

Natalie laughed and took off her apron, hanging it on the hook, "Trust me, if I can help it, I'll avoid them all. Italian men are arrogant and ostentatious, especially the newer generation. To them status is more important than common decency."

She knew all too well how Italian men operated. Her father was a typical example. Since she can remember, her mother had to always do as she was told. And even though her mother hardly ever complained, she knew that, that was not the life she would want for herself.

If she ever did marry, it would be to a gentle soul who gave as much as he took. She would marry a man with a heart of gold and a love for food, one who would love her with her extra padding and all.

"Belinda, the shuttle is here," her father called from the office.

"Coming papa," she responded and hugged Natalie, "If you need anything, just email me, I'll be online."

"Stop fussing so much, we'll be fine and I promise you, El Pescore will still be standing when you get back."

She glanced around the kitchen one last time and then took her purse and headed out to the shuttle. Maybe this holiday was just I need, she the shuttle pulled away. She was going to enjoy herself and come back refreshed and ready to take the bull by the horns.

Chapter 3

It's been a while since she last visited Palermo, but even after all these years nothing much had changed. There were still many thriving market places in nearly every corner and small apartments were stacked high above the streets giving their occupants a bird's eye view of the hustle and bustle below.

They exited Palermo, leaving behind the crowded streets and made their way along the winding road through the vineyards towards *Villa Valentina Paci*. She couldn't help but notice her father's mood deteriorate the closer they got to their destination, it was as if he was drawn into himself more now than ever before.

"Everything okay papa?" she asked placing her hand on his.

"Of course *tesoro*, why do you ask?" he said and smiled.

"You just seem quiet, that's all."

"It's been a long trip, I'm just tired," he said and squeezed her hand.

It was a valid reason but she couldn't help but concern herself over his wellbeing.

As they approached the gate to the Villa, she noticed the two armed men on either side of the entrance as the gate automatically opened. Their presence sent a cold shiver down her spine. *Why on earth would Mr. Angelino have armed guards?* She wondered briefly. They finally pulled up to the front of the magnificent Sicilian styled house with its rustic yet modern appearance. And although they were well off, and lived in a luxurious house in the suburbs in NY, this place was far grander than the house they owned.

It wasn't long before two men exited the house. The older one of the two, presumably her father's old friend Stefano, was the first to rush down the stairs to greet them.

"*Vicchio amico*, I'm glad you finally came to visit. It's been too long," he greeted and kissed her father on his cheeks, "This must be your be your lovely daughter."

"Stefano, old friend, it has been long," her father greeted in return and then stepped back, "Belinda, this is Stefano Angelo, and is his son Louis."

Belinda smiled, "It's a pleasure to meet you," she said softly trying not to pay too much attention to Louis. She had to mentally force herself not to look at him in an attempt to calm her frantic heart.

Natalie was right, Italian men were hunks, and this one was no exception. He had this air of grandeur that made the sun look like a fading lamp in the fog. Dressed in a suit, with his hair impeccably styled, he looked like he stepped out of a fashion magazine. And if his mere presence wasn't enough, he took her hand in his, which sent a spark of desire shooting through her body.

"*Bella*," he said and then brought her hand to his lips, "what a pleasure to finally meet you again. I've heard so much about you."

She was quite surprised by his remark and the fact that she was being discussed at all, since she had no real memory of meeting him when she was younger.

"I trust it was all positive?" she said smiling and withdrew her hand.

"Nothing negative can be said about such a beautiful creature," he remarked and stepped aside as his father led them into the house.

Not only was he good looking but he could charm a bird out of a tree, she thought feeling his eyes burn into her back. She couldn't wait to tell Natalie about Prince Charming. It'll give her a good laugh.

One of the servants of the house came and collected their luggage and the four of them made their way through the house to the terrace. The house was even more beautiful on the inside, and its casual layouts evoked an Old World charm. The interior decorator clearly had an inherent eye for design and the incredibly refined mosaics that adorned the walls simply captivated her.

Chapter 4

Louis studied his unsuspecting soon-to-be-bride as she scrutinized the food and he couldn't help but smile. She was literally picking at every morsel of food analyzing the textures and the tastes, most likely looking for cooking flaws.

"Is the food to your liking?" he asked her and immediately drew her attention.

"Oh it is, you must have a very skilled chef," she said smiling, and although he could see the slight blush in her cheeks, she kept her poise.

"I believe you are a master chef back in America," he stated and took a sip of his wine.

"Hardly a master, but I know my way around the kitchen and I know what people like to eat," she said confidently.

She isn't exactly my type, he thought as he studied her. She was on the shorter side, and curvy, a complete contrast to the women that normally shared his bed. He also preferred blondes; she had long black curly hair that fell loosely over her shoulders and down her back. She was a little too average for his liking, but even so, she was not unsightly. He could definitely work with this and once she was his wife, he would ensure that she was treated to a makeover.

He heard her clear her throat and realized she was staring at him. Caught red handed he lifted his glass to his lips and kept eye contact with her over the brim of the glass until she averted her gaze. *Shy – that was nothing short of adorable,* he thought and smiled.

"Louis, why don't you go show Belinda the winery, I'm sure she would love to see it?" his father suggested. And so it starts, the game of ultimate seduction. He still had no idea why his father insisted on taking her as his bride. But going against his father's wishes was not a chance he was willing to take. Besides, if he grew tired of her nothing would stop him of having a string of very willing mistresses.

He stood up and walked around the table then held out his hand for her, "Would you like to see the winery, *signora*?" he asked.

Instead of taking his hand she shifted her chair back and got up then kissed her father on his forehead and whispered something in his ear. She was rather mysterious. Just when he thought she was a shy and insecure mouse, who would easily be swayed, she acted the complete opposite, strong willed and determined.

"I've always been intrigued by wineries," she said as they walked down the pebbled path.

"It is an art to create the perfect wine. It has been the essence and life source of our family for decades and is one of the most well-known brands in Italy. It started with my great grandfather who planted the first vineyard and it simply grew from there."

She was intrigued by the whole process, and although she did have some knowledge of how wine was made, she didn't know the details of how red wine was made differently from white wine. He explained to her that red wine is made from the pulp by fermenting the grapes with their skins, while white wine is made by fermenting the juices. He showed her the fermentation process and then took her through to where the grapes were being foot trodden, and for a moment she wanted to kick her shoes off and join the workers.

They spent most of the afternoon in the cellar where she got to taste some of the wines, and by nightfall, she felt all but normal. Her head was spinning a little and she felt braver than usual, even a little flirtatious.

"So, do you have a girl friend?" she asked boldly as she wrapped her arms around one of the poles in the cellar. It was to have something to steady herself than anything else.

"That is a rather random question to ask a complete stranger," he said laughing. And his laughter sent a shiver through her.

"It's a normal question, I mean you have all this," she started and gestured with her hand, "Not to mention the looks and the charm, surely you have a woman who shares your bed?"

Woah, that's a little over the top Belinda, she scolded herself as he threw his head back laughing.

But for the life of her, she could not control herself even if she wanted to. It was as if all her thoughts were about to pour out of her mouth like water from a burst water pipe.

"No *bella*, I have no woman sharing my bed. Not yet anyway," he teased standing far too close for comfort.

She inhaled deeply and then breathed out, blowing her hair away from her forehead. "I'm sorry, it was a little rude asking you such a private question. It must be the wine that is influencing my filters," she apologized and moved away from him, half stumbling until she leaned against one of the wine barrels.

He moved closer as if she was his prey and as he reached out he ran his fingers up her bare arm, "It appears that the truth serum is working as expected," he said huskily.

"I-I'm n-not much of a t-truth serum fan," she stammered and slipped out from under his burning gaze and scooted along the wall. He was just far too intense.

Chapter 5

There was something about her innocence that attracted him on a level he was not accustomed to. And for reasons beyond his understanding, he had to have a taste of this forbidden fruit. He discarded the physical attraction and played it off as a ploy to seduce her into marrying him. This was all just business, and in his world, business always mixed with pleasure. So, while he is on this mission to claim her hand in marriage, he may as well enjoy the ride.

He boxed her in between his arms and blocked her escape path, "You are not afraid of me, are you?" he asked tilting her chin up, forcing her to look into his eyes.

"N-no, I'm not," she whispered nervously.

"Good," he said as he lowered his lips to hers. He kissed the corners of her mouth gently at first and then he wrapped one arm around her waist, pulling her up against him.

Her breath mixed with the woody scent of matured wine filled his lungs as she let out a huff of air parting her lips involuntarily. That was all he needed, her approval. He slanted his lips against hers and swept his tongue along het bottom lip and into her mouth. At first take, it was as if her jaw was locked, but as his tongue kept teasing hers, she relaxed and she returned his kiss. He slipped his other hand under her long tresses of hair and cupped the back of her neck as he deepened the kiss, drawing out a soft moan from her. This was more potent than he expected he suddenly realized as his body responded to hers. Should he go all the way now, or slowly draw her into his world, hook line and sinker?

Unable to think straight with the urgency of his arousal soaring to new heights, he dropped his hands to her hips and effortlessly lifted her unto a barrel. But the moment he did this, she protested and tore her lips away.

"This isn't right, I hardly know you," she uttered breathlessly.

"*Bello*, we are two adults, what are you worried about?" he asked, circling his thumbs on the inside of her knees where he stood between her legs.

"Louis, please let me go," she pleaded but made no attempt to move.

"This is your *no*, when you really mean to say *yes*?" he asked teasingly as he tried to kiss her again, but she turned her head away.

"I-I'm not ready for this," she said and pushed his hands away, "I've never..."

"Never, what?" he asked curiously as he tilted her chin up to look into her eyes, "Kissed in a winery?"

His arousal was painful and he was trying really hard to keep this as light hearted as possible. Usually he had more control than this.

"Kissed? No, I mean... ugh," she huffed and shoved him away from her then slid off the barrel, "I don't make it a habit of having sex with men I hardly know," she spat out and fixed her dress, "what would you think of me if I were to throw myself at you like a whore?"

This was the closest thing to a cold shower he could have asked for. Did she genuinely think that giving of herself will put her in the same class as a cheap whore? He cursed himself mentally but remained composed, and despite his raging desire he smiled and reached for her hand, then turned it over and kissed the inside of her wrist.

"I suppose we should start to work towards that second date then," he said and then let go of her hand.

"Come, I'm sure everyone is wondering where we disappeared to."

That was the quickest Samantha ever sobered up. One moment her head was spinning with wine and the next Louis was kissing her. And it was not just any kiss. It was the type of kiss that made your toes curl and your knees buckle. But everything was happening too soon. She came here thinking it would be a visit, hardly expecting to meet such a man like Louis. Not to mention one who would consider her worthy of his company.

Back home she was always the odd one out, with her friends landing all the hot guys. She was the designated driver who didn't drink, didn't fool around and made sure everyone got home safe and sound. She was also last on the picking list when it came to the men in her circles.

She followed Louis back to the Villa and tried to make sense of it all, but with him in front of her, larger than life, it was near impossible. The way his muscles flexed under his white dress shirt when he walked was simply hypnotizing, not to mention the way his back tapered down to his waist. He was the epitome of Anteros himself, the Italian god of love and passion. And she was in serious trouble.

Chapter 6

The week flew by and every day Belinda spent in Louis' company she slowly warmed up to him. Some days they would casually spent time together; steal a chaste kiss or two. Other days, she would merely sit by and watch how he ran the business. On those days, she saw a different side of him, one she wasn't sure she liked. He was demanding, refusing to take no for an answer. Although she did not quite agree with his methods, she respected him. Besides, soon she will go back to New York, to her own restaurant doing what she loved.

She was seated on one of the sofas on the terrace waiting for Louis to fetch her and take her into town when her father came to sit beside her. Again, she noticed the somber expression that made him look years his age.

"Papa, I'm worried about you, you don't look well," she said as she shifted closer resting her head on his shoulder.

"I'm perfectly fine, you fuss like your mother," he said and took her hand in his.

Belinda laughed and kissed his cheek, "I am a chip off the old block. Someone must see to it that you are happy and healthy."

"I'm a grown man," he said and there was a brief silence, before he spoke again.

"Louis is a good man," he started and she instantly knew where this was heading.

"He's a fine man, just a pity he's all the way out here."

Her father turned to her and took both her hands in his, "Belinda, I'm not getting any younger; I wish that you will marry before my time passes on earth."

Woah where did that come from, she wondered as she studied her father. He can't possibly consider her marrying Louis. Her life was in New York and even if Louis was marriage material, she would never give up El Pescore.

"Oh papa, that's utter nonsense. You are still as strong as a stallion. And the day I marry and have children you will be there to witness it in the flesh," she reassured him.

"You and Louis get on well," he said and looked into the distance as if he had more to say.

What was the sudden interest in Louis, and why did she suddenly feel a heavy weight settle in the pit of her stomach? She glanced across the lawn to where Louis was pacing up and down talking on his cell. *This is just a fling, nothing more*, she told herself and smiled at her father.

"We get on well papa, he's a good man, but I just don't think marriage is in his immediate future."

Her father was silent and the heavy weight that slowly settled in the pit of her stomach now consumed all her internal organs including her heart.

Papa is just showing concern and sharing his hopes, she convinced herself, but this gnawing voice in the back of her mind kept asking her, *what was really going on*. She looked up and noticed Louis crossing the lawn towards them and as he drew nearer her father got up and kissed her forehead.

"I must go meet with Stefano," he said then nodded at Louis then headed back into the house.

She was still looking at her father when Louis came to sit next to her and wrapped his arm around her, kissing the nape of her neck, "You look troubled," he said nuzzling her neck.

"Oh no I'm fine," she said smiling, "it's just papa, he seems very depressed lately."

"I'm sure he will be fine," Louis said and took her hand, "if you want, I can talk to him."

She laughed softly and shook her head, "No that won't be necessary, I'm sure he's just home sick."

"That might be it," he said and pulled her to her feet. "So are you ready to go to town?"

"*Si*, I'm ready!" she said laughing and just like that her mood shifted. Louis knew exactly how to make her feel better, and for a moment she wondered, *what if...*

Chapter 7

They spent most of the day in town, and Louis was not shy to flash his credit card either and he went out of his way to spoil her. Although she felt somewhat guilty, she simply convinced herself to enjoy it while it lasts. One more week and she will be back at the grind stone and this entire period of her life would be over.

"We're just in time for dinner," he said as they entered the house.

The rich aroma of sautéing onions, butter and roast beef filled the air and her stomach rumbled loud enough for her to hear it.

"Well my stomach has spoken, I'm starving," she giggled and led the way to the dinner table, but her appetite soon faded when she detected the somber mood that hung heavily in the air. She glanced at her father, then at Stefano, but neither of the two said a word. When Louis entered, he also suddenly became withdrawn and quiet. *Maybe she was just imagining things* she thought and sat down when Louis pulled her chair out for her.

Stefano mumbled something in Italian under his breath, which she couldn't quite hear, but whatever it was, it clearly annoyed Louis. *Did his father not approve of the fact that he spent so much time with her,* she wondered briefly. But as the whispers became more urgent the mood catapulted into a driven force of negativity.

"I did not raise a coward for a son," Stefano piped up loudly.

"I told you I will get it done," Louis responded, and shoved his plate away from him.

She looked towards her father where he sat with a serious expression that troubled his face and she could stand it no longer.

"Excuse me, but what's going on?"

"We will talk after dinner," Louis said in an icy tone.

"No! We will talk now. This cannot wait any longer," his father demanded.

What on earth was going on here? Just a few minutes ago, this place was buzzing with excitement, now it felt like the grim reaper was about to collect his souls.

"Now is not the time," Louis said through gritted teeth as he stood up and glared at his father.

"No other time is better."

"Enough!" It was her father who spoke aloud finally.

"Belinda, you will marry Louis in a week's time," her father ordered.

She looked from one to the other, trying to determine if she heard correctly.

"Excuse me?" she asked in a shrill voice, "did I hear you correctly?"

"You heard me, in a week you will marry Louis," her father said flatly.

She could not believe her ears, her own father literally just ordered her to marry Louis. *This cannot be happening,* she thought as she desperately grasped for a response in the recesses of her mind.

"Papa, I don't even know him, how can you expect me to do such a thing?" she said in disbelief, but this time Stefano stood up.

"This is not a request, your parents promised you to my son when you were just a *bambino*, and the time has come for them to be true to their word," he said flatly.

"What?!" both Belinda and Louis exclaimed at the same time.

She glared at her father and then at Stefano. How could her father have made such a promise on her behalf? And as the initial shock subsided, anger and rage replaced that empty space in her soul.

"You cannot make me marry a man I hardly know! What about love and commitment where does that fit into the picture..." she started but just then Louis placed his hand over hers.

She whipped her head around and glared at him, "And you! You knew all about this arrangement, didn't you?" she retorted and laughed incredulously, "this was all just a game to you wasn't it?"

"Belinda..." Louis said, but she wouldn't let him talk.

"All this time, charming me, kissing me, taking me out shopping, it was all a ploy for you to get me to marry you, wasn't it?"

Tears were pooling in her eyes, but they were not because of sadness, they were filled with bitterness and anger.

"That's enough," Stefano roared as he shoved his chair back across the floor, "You will marry my son and that is final."

She glared at Stefano with utter hatred, wishing she could scratch his eyes out, but then she caught a glance of her father's worried gaze. Louis had also stood up and was trying to drag her away from the dinner table, but she would have none of it and she tugged her arm free.

"You're acting like a bunch of hooligans, my god, this is not the mafia, what is wrong with all of you?" she cried out, but the silence she was greeted with was so deafening you could hear a pin drop. She looked at her father, then at Stefano and lastly, at

Louis. All three with their eyes cast down liked accused criminals. And then it hit her. *Impossible,* she thought, *they can't possibly be a part of the mafia.*

"Oh god papa, tell me it isn't true?" she pleaded as the room started to spin. "Please papa, don't make me do this," she begged and before she could utter another word, the room went completely black.

Louis caught Belinda just as she toppled over and without as much as a glance at the two older men he carried her upstairs to her room. This was a bad idea from the start and right now he hated himself. He gently laid her down on her bed and instructed one of the servants to keep an eye on her and then headed back downstairs.

"*Cosa stavi pensando*!" he ground out as he confronted his father, "I told you I would handle this, I do not see the point of rushing such a decision."

"The girl will be fine once she comes to terms with everything," his father said callously.

"Why the sudden rush?" he demanded looking from his father to Gino.

"It is the only way we can strengthen our ties in the United States. With our families united, we'll be the most prominent and the most influential family, a true force to be reckoned with," his father stated.

"At the cost of your daughter's happiness?" he bit out turning his attention to Gino.

"We have all had to sacrifice one thing or the other Louis; it's a small price to pay."

Unbelievable! He couldn't comprehend how her father was capable of betraying his own daughter like that.

He looked at them for a moment then straightened up.

"From now on, you will both stay out of our affairs. To claim her hand in marriage would need a miracle, and I hope for your sakes that God will be kind enough to soften her heart, so I hope you visit confession before Sunday mass."

Furious with his father, Gino and himself, he stormed out. He needed to figure out how he was going to fix this.

Chapter 8

The next day Belinda was packed and ready to leave. She wanted nothing to do with her father, and as far as the Angelinos were concerned, they could all burn in hell. She was not some possession to be put on auction for the next best bidder. She was a woman in her own right.

While standing at the window, waiting for a cab to arrive she replayed every single detail of the past week. What hurt even more than the betrayal of her father, was the fact that Louis had no affection towards her. All this time he simply baited her, just so that he could reel her in like a fish. She was nothing but a business deal.

There was a slight knock on the door, which she ignored, just like the knock from earlier that happened to be a servant bringing her breakfast, which had gone untouched. There was another knock, and when she didn't answer the door opened slowly.

"Belinda, can we talk?"

Speak of the devil! She thought as she glared at Louis, she had nothing to say to him other than the fact that she hated him.

"I was not aware of the arrangement between our parents, you have to believe me," he said and came to stand next to her, "that was a surprise to me too."

She tried to tune him out and shifted her weight leaning away from him. Even with his betrayal, her body still reacted to his closeness and her heart cramped painfully. Her attraction to him just made her hate him more.

"Say something," he said quietly.

She could sense that his eyes were pinned on her but just then, and much to her relief, she saw the cab arriving.

"I have nothing to say to you Louis," she said bitterly and gathered her luggage. But Louis was quick to stop her from taking another step and blocked her way.

"You're not the only one who has been forced into doing things you don't want to do. And I am just as caught up in this mess as you are."

She glared at him and dropped her bags to the floor, "Let's get one thing straight, NO one on this god forsaken earth is going to tell me how to live my life, least of all tell me who I will and will not marry. I am done with these games so I suggest you step aside."

She was taken aback when Louis suddenly laughed incredulously.

"I'm glad you find this so amusing." she scowled.

The one moment Louis was laughing, and the next he had a deadpan look on his face with his lips tightly pursed. She could see the tiny muscle flex in his jaw, and when he stepped forward and stood so close she could feel his breath fan his face, she felt scared for the first time.

"You do not choose your family in the mafia, you're born into it tesorina, and once you are a part of them, everything you own becomes theirs. Your business, your home even your *bambinos* and trust me there is no way out of it. So if you want the brutal truth, here it is. We are getting married, whether you like it or not."

Impulsively Belinda raised her hand to slap him in the face, but he gripped her wrist firmly and tugged her against him and with his lips pressed against her hair, he whispered, *"La calma è la virtù dei forti – the calm is the virtue of the strong."*

He left her with those words, which at that very moment meant absolutely nothing to her. When she looked back out the window, she saw the cab driving out of the gates.

Chapter 9

Belinda spent the next two days locked in her room, refusing to talk to her father or to Louis. Her life as she knew it was over. She was part of the mafia now, and organized crime was going to be a part of her future. She supposed she was always a part of it, just ignorant of her role. She was surprised that no-one came to put a tracking bracelet on her ankle to track her every move, since she should be considered a flight risk. If she had it her way, she would be sneaking out in the dead of night to flee this god forsaken fortress.

She took her out her laptop and rested it on her lap, and while she waited for it to start up, she couldn't help but wonder if they were screening her calls and internet activity. *If they were, then tuff luck,* she thought as she logged into her E-mail account. She had nothing to hide, and she sure as hell would not let anyone intimidate her.

The first email that loaded was from Natalie. She clicked on it hoping that hearing from her friend would improve her mood somewhat.

Hey Bee

When did we get a new accountant? Some guy rocked up at the restaurant saying that some Louis Angelino sent him. I don't know what's happening.

Cheers Nat

She took a few steady breaths to calm herself; Louis didn't lie when he said that the mafia owns everything. She tucked her bottom lip under her teeth and hit reply.

Hey Nat

Long story, I'll update you as soon as I can.

My stay here in Italy has been extended, but I'll keep you posted.

Love Bee

She couldn't really admit on e-mail that she was now a member of the mafia, forced to marry the Consigliere of the Angelino family and was being held hostage. *What an utter mess,* she thought as she shut her laptop. She really had no say in the matter, she had nowhere to run and knowing how the mafia operated, she had two choices. She could fight them, or accept her fate. But inevitably the mafia will win.

Louis stood in the study looking out the window, by now he was sure that Belinda had come to terms with her fate, much like he had to when he was only eighteen. Being forced to marry someone against her will, and the fact that his father omitted to tell him about the promise made when he was only six years old infuriated him. Needless to say, there was no denying the fact that he was attracted to Belinda, something he hardly expected to happen.

During the time he spent with her before the house of cards came tumbling down, he got to know a confident woman, one who challenged him like none of the others ever did. And albeit he had prior notions to transform her into a supermodel to his liking, he ended up liking her just the way she was. The fact remained, they will be married and they will have to learn to live with each other, there was simply no other choice. He could only hope that she would learn to accept it, and maybe by some miracle, she might learn to love him despite his role in betraying her.

The driveway was starting to fill up with cars, family and friends from surrounding towns were all gathering to meet his fiancée thanks to his father and Gino. He rubbed his forehead and closed his eyes. He was going to have to talk to Belinda before they faced they music.

When he got to her door, he knocked but knowing that she would not answer, he pushed the door open slightly. She was standing in front of the full-length mirror trying to put on her necklace.

"I suppose I have to play the role of the dutiful fiancée now," she said blankly.

He didn't reply, simply walked over to her and took the necklace from her, fastening the clasp.

"It doesn't have to be all that unpleasant," he said as he watched her in the reflection of the mirror, "we had real chemistry before all this happened, all is not lost."

"Unfortunately betrayal is the only truth between us. I can play the role Louis, but I cannot forget or forgive the betrayal," she stated and turned to face him.

The truth was like a bitter wine that dried his throat and turned his stomach. But here she stood before him and he couldn't ignore the way his body responded to her closeness. The steeliness in her hazel eyes spoke volumes of confidence fueled by anger, she was a determined and strong woman who will not only fit into his life, but become his life. The realization struck him like a lightning bolt and he cupped her face.

"*Tesoro*, this is not easy, but I will promise you this. I will be devoted to you always, I am a man of my word, and if it takes a lifetime to get you to forgive my betrayal, it's a lifetime worth living,"

Belinda was stunned into silence at his words and even though she was opposed to this arrangement she could not deny the attraction she felt towards him. *What if this turned out better than she expected?* She thought searching his eyes. She licked her lips and saw his eyes drop to her mouth. Her body and heart was at war with her mind.

"Don't make promises you can't keep," she said softly and stood on her toes to place a kiss on his cheek, then whispered; "liars make the best promises."

Chapter 10

She turned to walk to the door, but Louis grabbed her by her arm and tugged her roughly against him. And when his lips met hers, an uncontrollable moan escaped her and she simply slumped against him in surrender. She may not agree with the ways of their families, but that didn't mean she had to ignore the obvious sexual tension that had been escalating between them from day one. And if she was going to play the part of the Mafia Consigliere's wife, she may as well have fun doing so. She returned his kiss with such zeal she could have easily convinced herself that this was something more than a physical desire between two consenting adults.

Louis groaned and cursed in Italian and walked her back until her legs hit the bed and she flopped down on it. The desire she saw in his eyes ignited the same desire in her. He tugged at his shirt buttons and in no time shrugged his shirt off, tossing it aside. She followed suit taking her dress off and lay before him. Only wearing her lingerie.

"Mozzagiato," he said as he shoved his pants down over his hips while toeing his shoes off, "you are a goddess."

"Keep up the flattery, and I might consider forgiving you," she said wickedly and slid her hand around the back of his neck pulling him in for a kiss. His wedged his knee between her thighs and leaned over her supporting his weight with one arm, while he moved his other hand down to cup her breast.

"If flattery is all it takes, consider it done," he teased and dropped a string of kisses from the corner of her mouth, along her jaw and to the nape of her neck. His fingers curled around the lace of her bra tugging the one cup down to expose her breast, and then he latched onto her aching tip, sucking and swirling it in his mouth.

"Oh!" she cried out and threaded her fingers through his hair clinging unto his head. *I'm in so much trouble,* she thought and arched her back, pressing into him. Sleeping with the enemy had a whole new meaning all of a sudden.

Louis could hardly control himself as Belinda ground her body against his, she was so responsive, and the confidence that radiated from her was like a radioactive force consuming him. He moved his attention from her one breast to the other, biting her taut nipple through the lace of her bra eliciting a moan from her.

"*Ti desidero*," he whispered against her heated skin, "from the first day I saw you, *mia dolce*."

"The feeling is mutual," she said breathlessly.

He took his sweet time exploring every inch of her body, from her ample breasts to her curvy hips. And as he peeled her panties down her legs he knew he could no longer hold back.

"*Apri le gambe*," he demanded as he met her eyes, and she willingly spread herself open for him. *God help me*, he thought as he nipped nuzzled her neck sliding one hand down to cup her mound. She was soft and wet, her desire for him palpable, and as he rolled the pad of his middle finger over her clit she cried out dragging her nails across his skin.

He teased her a while longer, until her body was writing beneath him and when he finally moved himself into position, she wrapped her legs around his, pulling him into her.

"*Cazzo!*" he cried out as he drove his length into her wetness. Nothing could compare to what he was experiencing this very minute, and with each thrust into her, she met him. Stroke after stroke, her hips rose to meet his like an erotic dance between two lovers.

Between his grunts and groans he heard her moan his name, pleading with him not to stop. The way she vocalized her desires was a complete turn on, and he was edging dangerously close to his climax. As he reached down where their bodies met, he found her clit. All it took was a single touch to send her crashing over the edge and as her body shook and her nails dug into his skin, he surrendered and spilled himself into her. He lay on top of her for a few seconds before he rolled over unto his side, propping his head on his hand, admiring her where she lay still with her eyes closed. A smile tugged at the corner of her full lips, and he bent his head down and kissed her.

"Does this mean I am forgiven?" he whispered huskily and kissed her shoulder.

"No," she said and scooted to the edge of the bed, "but maybe if you do this again tomorrow, I will reconsider."

He chuckled and got off the bed reaching for his pants, then removed a small black box from the pocket.

"How about this?" he said and flipped open the lid exposing a diamond ring.

She smirked and reached for the ring then slid it on her ring finger, and without a word she gathered her dress and underwear and walked through to the bathroom closing the door behind her.

She was a complex creature, he thought with a grin as he too got dressed and headed downstairs.

Chapter 11

Belinda stood at the top of the stairs studying all the guests. She knew the organization was large but she couldn't help but wonder how many of these people were unsuspecting pawns unaware of the fact that the Angelinos and Benedettis were a part of this criminal organization.

Within a matter of two weeks she went from an ordinary woman to one forced to embrace her place in the mafia. If she was going to survive this, she was going to have to be strong and make her mark in society.

She tilted her chin defiantly and mechanically put one foot in front of the other as she descended the stairs. Her eyes locked on Louis as he stood at the bottom of the staircase. As she reached him, her father appeared alongside Stefano but she simply nodded at them both.

It was Stefano who announced the engagement and the pretense of it all was sickening, but she remained composed nonetheless. She had a few tricks up her sleeve, and with her position in such a powerful family at the side of Don Angelino's son, she was going to make this work to benefit her.

The evening soon drew to a close. Her father approached her on a few occasions but never quite spoke to her. At times her heart ached to reconcile with him, but she shut her emotions down. She was no longer going to be this timid soul who allowed others to walk right over her.

"Did you enjoy the evening?" Louis asked as he came to stand beside her after the last of the guests exited the house.

"It was pleasant," she said and sighed softly.

"Yes it was," he said and then took her hand in his, "you should to speak with your father."

She rolled her eyes and withdrew her hand from his, "I have nothing to say to him."

"Belinda, you can't shut him out forever."

"You want to bet on that?" she said bitterly, "In due time I might talk with him again, but right now, I want him to wallow in self-pity and reflect on his actions."

He took her by her shoulders and tilted her chin up, "Life is too short to harbor hatred, and the woman I met two weeks ago would never have been so callous."

"Well that woman died," she said blankly.

She simply had no choice but to toughen up, the only way she knew how. She had to feel nothing, allow no sadness, hurt or love to cloud her judgement. If that meant shutting everyone in her life out and pretending to be a cruel hard woman, then so be it.

A commotion outside drew their attention and Louis was the first to go and investigate, with her following closely. A small crowd of guests who still remained outside were huddled together in a group near the fountain. She shoved her way through the crowd to see what was going on and when she saw her father laying on the ground her heart stopped.

"Papa!" she cried out and dropped to her knees next to him, "papa!"

Louis was beside her immediately feeling for a pulse and checking his breathing, "I think it's a heart attack, I can't find a pulse."

"No!" she cried as horror gripped her heart, "Help him Louis!" she pleaded as tears streamed down her face. He immediately started CPR while Stephano called for an ambulance. Ten minutes later, her father was on his way to the hospital and Louis was driving like the devil himself following the ambulance.

At the hospital everyone gathered in the waiting room. Louis was seated next to Belinda trying to consoler her. He knew that if her father did not pull through she would blame herself for the rest of her life.

"Let's go and get some coffee," he said and took her hand.

"I don't want coffee," she mumbled.

"It will do you good, come," he insisted.

This time she didn't object when he pulled her to her feet, and led her to the cafeteria. Seated across from her at one of the small tables, he studied her intently.

"You shouldn't blame yourself, these things happen when we least expect it. For such a severe heart attack, he was probably sick for a long time."

"I want Natalie to run El Pescore," she said changing the subject completely.

"Belinda, business can be discussed at another time," he said and took a sip of his coffee.

"No, it can't. By Friday I'll be Mrs. Angelino-Benedetti, I know you have already acquired a new accountant for the restaurant without consulting with me, so now is as good a time as ever."

He cursed inwardly. His father had the very bad habit to stick his nose in everyone's business. He wasn't even aware of this change at El Pescore. The agreement was that the restaurant will remain unchanged. There was something dubious going on, not that it was any different from any of the other business deals his father was involved in. But for the sake of peace he agreed with her and reassured her that Natalie will be the manager in her absence.

"Miss Benedetti?" a somber voice spoke next to them. It was the doctor and the expression on his face was grave.

"I'm sorry we did all we could, but the damage to his heart was too severe."

Louis met her gaze and she hardly blinked. Simply closed her eyes and took a deep breath, then stood up and walked out of the cafeteria.

Chapter 12

A few weeks later Belinda sat in the confession booth at the Catholic Church and covered her head with her scarf. There were so many questions that remained unanswered and she needed a sign, any sign to tell her she was doing the right thing. The little door slid open and she sighed and kneeled.

"Bless me father for I have sinned, it's been four years since my last confession."

"Why has it been so long my child?" the priest asked.

"I don't know, I guess life just happened," she stated nervously.

"I see...so what would you like to confess today?"

"I'm not sure Father, it's quite complicated," she said suddenly having second thoughts about being here.

"Well, you do know that everything said here is completely confidential. So why don't you start at the beginning," he said in a modulated tone.

"I'm in a tricky situation; I have been forced to marry a man selected by my family."

"Do you know this man?"

"Yes Father, I know him well," she said not sure what else to say.

"How do you feel about the man?"

"I'm not sure, he's a kind man at times, but he's involved with..." she paused. Does she tell him about the fact that Louis is part of the mafia, and that she has no other option but to go through with this, or does she just ditch this whole confession and get on with life?

"What is he involved with?" the priest asked.

"I like him, I just don't know if I am ready to marry him," she said instead.

"But there is no love?"

"I don't know, it's all so very complicated," she started.

"I understand, but you know that God can give you guidance in situations like this, and I'm here to assist."

She was silent for a moment. This was a mistake, not even God can help her, she was stuck in a situation with no way out.

"I'm sorry Father, I just need a prayer."

"Of course my child," he said quietly and then followed with a short prayer for guidance.

"Thank you Father," she said biting back the sudden wave of nausea that hit her.

"Go in peace."

Belinda exited the booth and rushed to the nearest bathroom and dry-heaved over the toilet bowl. All this stress was starting to impact her health and if she didn't get a grip on life, she was going to end up in some mental hospital for severe depression.

She made her way out of the church and walked two blocks down to a café to get some coffee. The smell of freshly ground coffee assaulted her senses immediately but instead of liking it as she usually did, her stomach turned again and another wave of nausea hit her. *This was not stress* she thought and mentally calculated when she had her last period as she rushed out of the café. The tired spells, the nausea, everything pointed to one sure fact. She was pregnant!

As if her life wasn't complicated already, this took the cake. With the certainty of expecting Louis' child hanging heavily over her head, she slumped back against the concrete wall in the alley next to the café, and pressed her rosary against her lips. This cannot be happening, she kept telling herself as she fought the morning sickness. *You asked for a sign*, her thoughts echoed back at her.

"Impossible," she whispered to herself, "how can this be happening?"

She made her way back to the Villa fighting back the tears that threatened to spill. She was going to have to raise her child in the mafia, exposing him or her to the dark world she now lives in against her will and how was Louis going to take the news?

"Bella, I was getting worried," it was Louis voice that infiltrated her thoughts and her heart cramped painfully, "you're so pale, are you feeling ill?" he asked worriedly.

"I-I'm fine," she lied, plastering on a smile, "just tired, I think I need to go lay down."

"Of course," he said and immediately helped her to her room.

Her heart was racing and it felt as if something was squeezing the very air from her lungs as she walked up to her room. She had to tell him, but she didn't know how or when. The words were on the tip of her tongue, when she felt her stomach cramp. Without a word, she rushed into her room shutting the door in Louis face, and rushed to the bathroom. *This was an utter disaster*, she thought as she hunched over the toilet.

Chapter 13

Louis knew instantly that Belinda was not well, she was nervous and pale, and the way she bolted into her room had him worried. Concerned about her health he called their family doctor to see to her.

"Thank you for coming around Doctor, I'm quite concerned about my fiancé, she doesn't seem well. It could very well just be stress, but I'd prefer if you could take a look," he said as he walked alongside the doctor taking him upstairs.

"What are her symptoms?" the doctor asked.

"Tired, pale, overall she seems quite edgy. She recently lost her father as you know, and with the wedding drawing close, I think it might just be stress," he said quietly as they stood outside the room.

"Well that could very well be the case, but I'll take a look and run a few tests to make sure all is in order."

Louis opened the door for the doctor and then waited outside. This entire arrangement was handled incorrectly from day one, he thought as he paced in front of the door. He couldn't help but feel guilty for allowing his father to influence his choices like this. He should have refused the arrangement and taken the brunt of his father's rage instead of being such a coward. Now the woman he has slowly started to fall in love with is ill, and it was his fault. From the shy timid creature she was when he first met her, she now displayed the characteristics of a true Donna, unmoved and pokerfaced. She even refused to attend her father's funeral, who knows what was going on in her mind.

A little while later the doctor asked Louis to join him and he couldn't help but feel the immense sense of sadness as he looked down at Belinda where she lay staring out the window, her skin pale against the dark hair that framed her face.

"How is she?" he asked tentatively, taking her hand in his, surprised that she didn't pull away from him.

"She does show some signs of stress but it's very normal when a woman's body undergoes such extreme changes during pregnancy..." the doctor started.

"*Scusami*, pregnant?" he asked in disbelief.

"Yes, that is correct. She's about four weeks now," the doctor said and turned his attention to Belinda, "*Signora*, you would need to visit my rooms as soon as you feel up to it so that we can make sure everything is in order, but your blood pressure seems fine."

Louis stood in shock as he looked down at Belinda. This was the last thing he expected, he had assumed she was on birth control like most women should be in this day and age. How could she possibly be pregnant?

He walked the doctor to the door and let him find his own way out then came to sit beside her.

"Did you know you were pregnant?" he asked trying not to sound accusing.

"No, I didn't," she said without looking his way.

"Belinda, look at me. Were you not on birth control?" he asked trying to control his impatience.

She whipped her head around and glared at him, "No I was not. What seems to be the problem Louis, are you afraid that I might trick you into marrying me?" she bit out harshly.

"You know it's not like that," he countered.

"Do you think this is what I wanted, a baby born into the mafia!?" she said raising her voice.

"*Calmati*," he said and took a deep breath, "I'm sorry for upsetting you. I just didn't expect this," he said quietly.

"Well neither did I, so here we are. Getting married in a few days, and I'm having your baby. Instant family isn't that just brilliant," she bit out sarcastically.

"Bella, please don't stress yourself out, we can hold off with the wedding..."

"No, I will not walk down the aisle looking like a house or give anyone reason to think I am a promiscuous gold digger," she said bitterly, "we will wed as planned."

She had a point, everyone will think he is marrying her because she is with child, and the gossipmongers will have a field day. He just wished she could show more compassion, he wanted her the way she was when he first met her.

"As you will, *mio cara,* we will continue as planned."

"I'm tired," she said quietly turning her back on him.

"Get some rest, I'll bring you some food later, and we can talk about the wedding then."

He stood looking at her for a brief moment and then quietly left her to rest, closing the door behind him.

Although he didn't expect this to happen he couldn't help but feel a sense of pride knowing he was going to be a father. Maybe in time she would grow to love him and they would become a true family.

Chapter 14

Four weeks later...

With the passing of her father, the wedding was postponed but finally the inevitable day had arrived. She stood looking at herself in the mirror, the wedding dress was even more beautiful than she expected. Thankfully there were no signs of pregnancy as yet. Although her breasts were tender, she had gotten over most of her morning sickness which was a relief. To her surprise, Louis went out of his way to give her whatever her heart desired to make this day as perfect as it could possibly be. He even got Natalie to attend the wedding so that she could be the maid of honor.

"You look amazing Bee," Natalie said as she tucked some of the stray strands of hair back in place, "I still can't believe this is all happening so fast."

"It was love at first sight," she said quietly and stepped off the pedestal.

"You're so damn lucky."

You have no idea, she thought.

A slight knock on the door drew her attention but before Natalie could inquire who it was, Louis stepped into the room.

"Hey! You're not allowed to see the bride before the wedding!" she cried and tried to shove him back out the door.

"I have to see Belinda, it is of utmost importance."

Belinda looked at him and noticed the serious look on his face, then nodded at Natalie, "It's okay Nat, will you give us a moment?"

"Ugh, this is such bad luck," her friend mumbled and walked out of the room.

Louis could hardly take his eyes of Belinda, she was the most beautiful bride he had ever seen, and although he would want nothing more but to have her promise her entire life to him, he had a pressing matter to discuss. And this could very well be the end of this fairytale wedding.

"I had some of my men investigate an issue that has been on my mind for some time now," he started and walked to the window, "Remember when you mentioned the accountant?"

"Yes?" she said curiously.

"We'll I never made that arrangement, my father did. So I had him investigated."

He turned to her and took both her hands in his.

"It is true that our parents promised us to each other when we were just children, but my father had ulterior motives. You see, El Pescore has been a front for my father, it was the only way he could invest his money in the United States..." Louis started to explain. He told her how he found out about his father's business, and how he used El Pescore's Italian food supplier as a front to legitimize the movement of money from Italy to America.

Belinda was shocked to the core. All this time her pride and joy was a sham. She slowly sat down on the bed with a hundred and one questions flooding her mind.

"I want you to listen to me. I have already moved my father's assets away from your restaurant, and signed the business over into my name," Louis said as he stood on his haunches in front of her, "but my father will soon find out, and when he does all hell will break lose. The only way I can secure your safety is if you were my wife."

For a moment her mind went blank, but clarity soon descended on her and she looked at Louis with both determination and admiration. She knew that what he had done was dangerous but the fact that he did this for her must mean that he cared.

"Is El Pescore in danger of being closed down or destroyed?" she asked.

"No, with El Pescore no longer the front, it will be meaningless for him to pursue it and I will ensure that nothing happens to your restaurant or to your staff."

"Good, then I will marry you," she said quietly.

Louis stood up and dragged his hands through his hair, "That's just it. I don't want you to just marry me. I want you to *want* to marry me. I want our child to know that his parents care for each other."

That took her for a loop, and she wasn't quite sure she understood what he wanted. Over the past few weeks after her father's death, Louis was compassionate and understanding and somewhere between, *I hate you* and *I forgive you*, she fell in love with him, not to mention that she now carried his child. But it was a realization she opted to bury forever. It took her weeks to come to terms with the fact her love for him would be unrequited.

"You want me to *want* to marry you?" she asked tilting her head.

"*Si*, marriage without love is nothing but a business transaction," he said and kissed the palm of her hand. "I want our child to have a happy home."

When he did things like that she could not fault him. She wanted him and from his declaration he wanted her too. She sat for a moment and contemplated her future.

"Do you love me?" she asked.

"I didn't believe this to be possible, but you've changed me somehow. And knowing that I might marry a woman who does not love me made me reconsider..." he started and then came to sit next to her, "I am in love with you, which is why I don't want you to marry me if there is any doubt in your heart or mind."

She could feel the tears prick her eyes and she quickly blinked them away. For weeks she tried to be strong, harden her heart and show everyone that she was a force to be reckoned with. A woman who refused to let circumstance and tragedy weaken her, but now she could barely keep it together.

"I am in love with you too," she whispered.

"*Mio dolce amore,* then we shall marry and take this world by storm. I will protect you and our child all of my days."

Suddenly her walls crumbled down and a sob ripped through her chest. All her pent-up emotions like a raging river, broke the walls that she fought so hard to keep erected.

"Once we are married, I will go with you to New York, and we will start afresh there," he said as he cupped her face in his hands.

"What will happen when your father finds out about El Pescore?" she asked searching his eyes.

"Let me worry about that, *mio caro*, I'm his son, and you are now his daughter-in-law, he will find other ways to manage his business. I will help him set up a shelf company in the United States, one that will have no strings to El Pescore or the Benedetti's," he reassured her and then pressed his lips against her, kissing her softly.

***

After the wedding, they both left for New York to start their own family. Belinda accepted the fact that her life will never be the same, but with Louis by her side and their child on the way, she knew she could face any circumstance. After her father passed away, she assumed the position as the Donna Benedetti in the largest Mafia Family in the United States.

Louis earned his father's respect, despite the fact that he created a shelf company for his family, withdrawing El Pescore as the front for the mafia.

*****

THE END

Her Billionaire Boss's Baby

Chapter 1

"Order up!"

As a child, my Mom had always asked me, after every single cartoon or sitcom, what catch phrase I would like to respond to when I grew up. She always told me the best heroes always knew when they had to step up to the plate by a certain 'call to action' they would receive.

I never quite got around to answering her question, it was far too difficult for a kid to answer, I suspect, and I never really saw myself as a larger than life character to begin with. It's either you got it or you don't, right?

So I wasn't larger than life, but I was starting to feel like I was too large for my uniform as I stood up to respond to my call of duty. I tugged on my uniform to straighten out the creases that had set in from me sitting down and folding napkins. I looked down at myself, seeing the polyester hug onto my figure, and that reminded me so much of my Mother's figure. I always feared the day I would cross the line, where I didn't just weigh more than average.

I didn't have that much to worry about though, I wasn't getting any heavier. I spent most of my day serving people food, I hardly had time to eat any food myself, but I would have to tell my Dad to order me a new uniform anyway. This uniform was still too tight on me.

My dad and I were your modern-day partners in crime and the Baxter's Family Restaurant was our main gig. We've had a family restaurant in the middle of nowhere since I was a little girl and as much as my Mom filled me with fantasies of doing bigger things with my life, responding to some great catch phrase of a call, the semantic version of a bat signal perhaps, I found myself pretty content spending my days responding to my Dad's voice calling "Order up!".

Muleshoe, Texas, was a notoriously small town and our family restaurant was the cornerstone of its dining culture. As a little girl, it was great, from what I remember. I spent every evening helping my Mom clean tables and talking to the locals as they waited for their meals. Seeing as the town was so small, we knew every customer we had on a first name basis, and our restaurant was like an extended home to everyone in our town, and my Mom was virtually, I daresay, the town's ray of sunshine. All anyone had to do on a stressful, barren day was order the special at the Baxter's family restaurant and ask my Mom for five minutes of her time, and it would be all okay, and if it wasn't, all you had to do was add some Sangria to your order, we were the only place in town that stocked it. I liked to see my parents as small time heroes of a small-time city, and I gobbled up every chance to learn the ins and outs of the business. They always talked about how in their post-adolescence, when the world was but a stage and they had an infinite pool of dreams and potential to pick from, that they would dream of having a restaurant, and it elated me that they had being able to achieve their goals in their lifetime – especially now that Mom was gone.

It had only been a few years since my Mom had lost her fight with cancer, and that's when life really started to change. My Dad had vowed to her that he would keep their dream alive until his dying breath, but she had forced me to take a different kind of vow. Okay she didn't really force me, but she urged me not to stay in this small town forever – she told me a secret she had never shared with dad. Although she loved our little town of Muleshoe with all her heart, and loved every family she was connected to in it, she had always dreamed of seeing the world, or at least travelling to a bigger town, and she regretted dying without doing it. She asked me to find the courage in myself to explore what the world had to offer, and not limit myself to the family restaurant. She said it was made to let our dreams become a reality, not to hold us back. Of course, at the time this sounded almost ludicrous. She was supposed to get better! All that talk about death was superfluous and quite stifling, all she had to do was get better and we could all see the world. Together.

"Teresa! Did you hear me? Table seven's order is ready," the sound of my Dad's voice was stern, but still held its gentle tendencies. That's just the kind of guy he was, it was always difficult to keep a grudge against him.

"Sorry, Dad. Does this seem a little too tight to you?" I asked, tugging at the hemline of my dress. My dad called them 'traditional style uniforms' which was pretty much code for ancient and unattractive if you asked me.

"What are you talking about?" he asked, not even glancing at my uniform. He was too busy getting his act together for lunch hour. "The lunch rush is happening in ten minutes, and you need to be on top of your current tables. So, could you please take this food to the Martins?"

I sighed and grabbed the two plates out of the window, trying to push back down the rising levels of self-consciousness my shrinking dress was giving me. I noticed my Dad was smirking, and for the briefest moment I thought he might be mocking my dress in his head, until I realized he was just admiring his 'work'. Dad's *Masterpiece Meatloaf* was on the day's special board, and he was really proud of his recipe. Both plates were filled with a gracious amount of portions, along with mixed vegetables and a roll. He always kept things simple. He constantly reminded me that keeping things simple was what the locals wanted, every time I suggested a bit of a change to our almost archaic menu. The business had managed to stay profitable in this small town for over thirty-five years, so maybe he did have a point, but all it was going to take to give us a serious run for our money was a new restaurant with a new menu. I turned around with the Martin's orders and headed to their table.

The Martins, like most of the folk in this town, were a peaceful couple well into their twilight years. They just sat there, sipping on their hot tea and engaging in small talk about seeds for their garden, how good a job the painter did or whatever it was old couples considered small talk. They lived a few blocks down, so they were practically our neighbors. I had graduated high school with their grandson, Gavin. He had left our little town a few years back and Dean and Phyllis were the only members of that household left.

"Here you go," I smiled as I placed a plate in front of Phyllis. "Take it easy diving into the food now, we don't want another incident, now do we?" I teased Dean as I lay his meal in front of him.

"Don't worry about me, pumpkin!" Dean responded, smiling voraciously as he got ready to eat.

"Anything else you would like?" I asked as I arranged the napkins and cutlery the same way my Mom taught me all those years back.

"No, dear," said Dean in his earnest and elderly voice. "I'm ready to eat this meal up. How 'bout you Phyllis?" he glanced away from his meal for a split second, almost as if to register with his wife to show that he always remembered his love for her, even when faced with his favorite meal.

Phyllis gave a subtle roll of her eyes at Dean's feigned concern then shot me with a kind smile.

"Everything's fine, Teresa. Thank you." I nodded and stepped away from the table, but before I could get two steps away Phyllis called out to me, "Oh, Teresa."

"Yes?" I spun around. The way my dress moved brought back my over awareness of my size.

"I forgot to tell you. Gavin insisted I tell you he will be in town next weekend. He knows we spend a lot of time here and that you still work here."

"Oh," I responded. Gavin, huh? I wondered what his life was like, outside our small-town life. I hadn't seen the guy since we graduated, nor had I heard anything about him until this very moment. The little bits of detail I could recall all came from town gossip, which was rather inconclusive, people simply said he had gone to college. Nobody said what he went to do or where he went to do it. I was close to him as a kid because we lived on the same street, but we drifted apart when we entered high school. I was more into sports and he was more into Physics. That kind of stuff can make or break a friendship in high school. "How is he doing? I bet he's having a grand time with his big city family, isn't he?"

Phyllis chuckled a little. "Family? Gavin doesn't have any family except those of us he left here. That boy is married to his work, I tell you. Treats his contracts like babies, instead of having real children. I'm still trying to accept the fact that I won't have any great-grandchildren, but at least we made it this far, right Dean?" She looked at Dean, who was engrossed in his meal already and hardly paying any attention.

He swallowed his food and let his cutlery down for a moment. "Let the boy make his own choices, Phyllis. Each to their own. He don't wanna have kids? He shouldn't have kids then. Maybe one day some pretty city girl will take a liking to him and he'll buckle under the pressure of her goldilocks, but until then, we mind our own business."

"He's over forty, Dean. You focus on your meatloaf instead of wishing on the stars like that." Phyllis said. It was always amusing watching old couples squabble. No one ever won and no one ever lost, but they did it anyway. "You know the reason he's going to be in town is for the reunion. I'm sure you'll meet each other there."

The reunion. It had been weeks since the invitation popped up in my email, and I had completely forgotten about it. Attending my twenty-year high school reunion was not exactly on my to-do list. I must have pushed it to the back of my mind as soon as I had finished reading it because I had no interested whatsoever in attending it. Thinking about it in retrospect, it was a good call to discard it. Meeting all those people there, people like Gavin, was a whole load of unnecessary pressure. I couldn't imagine finding any pleasure in spending an entire evening with people that had all grown up in this town, just like me, that eventually left this town, unlike me. I chose to stay in this town because I liked this town. If no one else felt the same way I did, I couldn't bear having to explain myself and convincing twenty-three fellow graduates that I was happy here. Saying they all left might be a bit of an exaggeration on my part but the few people that did stay here still got involved with the corporate world, pursued big time white collar careers and spent their free time building families and creating legacies. I couldn't even remember the last time I had sex, so the chance of having babies was pretty low. I had lived the single woman life for a while now, and I wouldn't have anything in common with anyone at that reunion. I decided it was not worth my time at all.

Chapter 2

It was eight o'clock already. I was still at work, doing my part in the dinner rush, but the tempo was starting to slow down. Patricia, our other resident waitress, had it under control, so I decided I could call it a day. Brian, our number two cook, just behind Dad, was there to keep an eye on things with her. They were the most trustworthy employees you could ever hope for. They were both older than me, but not by much. Mom hired them some years ago, in a futile attempt to get the family more free time, but Dad still worked his daily shift, down to the last minute. What he did with the extra manpower was that he extended the restaurant's working hours. It went from being open eight hours a day to fifteen hours a day. It was starting to make sense as the days rolled by why my Mom wanted me to have a change of scenery and see what else life had to offer, but I had the nagging fear that it was too late for me. I didn't know what to fill my time with either, so I was working my full hours too. I must admit most of my effort was for my Dad, and his pay rates plus the tips made for a pretty decent income for an area like this, but he really was just an excuse for me. I couldn't think of anything else I could spend my days doing, so I just worked until I was too tired to go on. I was grateful for Patricia and Brian, they took the liberty of closing the diner every night. I was more of a morning girl and by this time on most days, there was a good chance I was passed out on the couch watching reruns.

At this point, all I wanted to do was have a nice little meal, fill myself up a nice bath and be over with my day. A flashback of my neglected fridge creeped through my mind and I realized it was much too late to stop by the grocery store. I wasn't even sure I had the energy to make a decent meal if I had the ingredients in my fridge but my belly was definitely going to disturb my sleep. I called in a favor with Brian and he willingly went to work on preparing me something to go. I debated what I was going to watch while eating it and preparing to pass out.

After a while Brian handed me my food. I grabbed my purse under the counter, and gave a wave to Patricia and some of the remaining punters on my way out. The jingle of the bell above the door announced my departure as I headed to my car parked out front. I couldn't wait to get home and go to bed.

Chapter 3

The next morning, I woke up to the sound of phone ringing relentlessly. It took me a few seconds to register what was happening. I looked down at myself. I was still wearing my waitress uniform. I had done this a million times before and was adding to my ever growing list of lazy habits I needed to quit. I reached over to my phone on the nightstand, right next to my now empty plate of food from the night before.

"Hello?" my voice was so raspy. Whoever was on the other line was definitely going to know that they woke me. I noticed a glass of water next to the phone. Score! High five to me for bringing a drink to bed, even though I should have remembered to take it before falling asleep.

"Hey pumpkin. Did I wake you?" My Dad was on the other line. I took a quick gulp of my water before I responded.

"Not really. What's up?"

"We're running low on tomatoes, think you can do something about that before you get here?" he asked.

"Yeah, sure. I'll pick up some on my way there."

He thanked me, but not before he went on a long and droned out explanation of what type of tomatoes I had to pick up, the same long explanation he had given me a million times before. The moment he took a breath, I chimed in.

"Okay, I've got it all handled. Don't worry, see you later Dad." I hang up and got to work preparing myself for the day.

***

"Teresa? Teresa Baxter, is that you?"

I was in the produce section of the local market searching for my Dad's perfect tomatoes when I heard my name. I turned around and found myself face to face with a middle aged woman and three young children hanging around her calves. I wasn't sure who would be questioning my identity in the market. I was here every other day and everyone knew me. I stared at the woman's face for a moment, but I couldn't place her anywhere in my head so I looked down at her children hoping to see some trait to tag them to a family bloodline I was familiar with.

"Yes. I'm Teresa."

"Teresa! It's Janet. We were in the same class for like, twelve years!"

Just then I remembered her. Time had taken a toll on her. The three young children that she seemed to be producing back to back, I mean they all looked under five, weren't helping her retain her youth either. She was almost unrecognizable. The last mental picture I had of her before this day was a vibrant and full of life girl back in high school. What had happened to her? She looked seriously run down. The grey was settling into her hair, and it wasn't just at her roots. Her weight gain made me feel comfortable in my own skin for the first time in a long time and the depression in her eyes far exceeded what I saw in Brian's the night before.

"Janet!" I said instinctively, trying to disguise my shock, or at least pass it off as a good type of shock, the happy to see her kind. "How are you?

What are you doing here?" It was genuinely nice to see someone from back in the day, but not really exciting.

"Teresa, it is so nice to see you after all this time. I'm back in town for a week. I'm staying with my parents. You should stop by. They would love to see you. I wouldn't have stayed the entire week, but you know, the reunion and all. Perfect timing, don't you think?" Teresa was enthusiastic. She gave off this vibe that made me wonder what she expected me to say her. At that particular moment, my brain felt like it was shutting down. "Teresa? Aren't you excited about the reunion?" she asked, grinning from ear to ear. "My parents will keep an eye on these little monsters for the evening, so I really plan to live it up!"

"Well, I hope you have a good time. Tell everyone hello for me," I said as I bagged up the two tomatoes I was holding. I gave her a sheepish smile as I prepared to bid her a good day, but the poor looked like I had just slapped her in the face. "What's wrong?" I asked.

"You're not going? You're one of the only people I was excited about coming back to party with. I don't have to a mom for one night and I imagined the perfect night would have you and me going out and living like we're in high school again, you know?" She was so excited it tugged at my heart a little that she thought my company would be so much pleasure. "You have to go! Pretty please? We need this. We need to go out and fun." Her emphasis on the needing part made me suspect that her children were really tiring her out.

"I'll think about it. Okay? It was really good to see you though, Janet, but I have to get going. My Dad is waiting for me at the restaurant. He needs tomatoes real bad," I said as I jiggled the plastic produce bag in my hand. "I'll see you later." I looked down and waved at the kids and headed in the other direction.

"You will see me soon, Teresa. Next weekend to be exact, at the reunion. You can't miss it!" She almost made it sound like a threat. As if something bad would happen to me if I didn't show up.

Chapter 4

"Got any plans for next Saturday?" I was back at the restaurant, and I was serving Sam another piece of apple pie.

"I never plan that far into the future. You know this. How can anyone make plans in Muleshoe, anyway?" Sam responded in his tender, loving voice.

Sam was an attractive guy. I had to give credit where it was due. He worked as a farmer on his family's land since graduating a few years before me. His father, Lonny Howard, was one of my favorite customers. That meant he was one of my best tippers. Sam and I had known each other for years, and occasionally we would hang out with each other from time to time as adults. Strictly platonic, but he was about the only male companionship I had even recognized existed in the last few years. Although our relationship never involved being romantic, I could tell that Sam cared for me, in a more than older loving brother kind of way. Of course, there were sometimes when his male instincts would remind him that I was not his blood sister and therefore he wouldn't be guilty of incestuous feelings, and my Dad, and even Patricia and Brian, would think we were romantically involved somehow, but that was just our friendly playfulness with each other. He and I had been very close friends all these years, and he was the one that was there for me during my Mom's passing.

"What would you say to going to my twenty-year high school reunion with me next Saturday?" I was trying to say it in a take it or leave it kind of way. The only reason I had even considered going now was because after encountered Janet at the market I figured the shock value she gave me was well worth the entertainment of a full night. I could see how everyone else turned out, good or bad, and I couldn't be that bad. I'd just changed in girth, nothing much else. "I mean, you don't have to go or anything. I was just wondering you wanted to. It might be fun to see everyone. Even if you were a few years older than them, you still hung out with a couple of us back in the day." I had to quit talking before I sounded too anxious.

"Sure. I'll go with you." Sam muffled as he stuffed a big piece of pie in his mouth. He grabbed his perfectly folded napkin and wiped the corners of his mouth. "Is it like prom? Do I have to buy you a corsage?" He smiled and looked down to get another heaping spoonful.

"Prom? No, why would you even say that? You've had reunions, it'll be the same as yours. What was yours like?" I was a little confused as to why he would say such an awkward thing about something that I figured was utterly mundane and commonplace among people older than me.

"Well," Sam proceeded, "most classes have five-year, ten-year reunions and so on. Most classes I know never just have a twenty-year class reunion, and as far as I can recall, your class has never had a single reunion until now. What's that all about?" I couldn't tell if he was being playful or sincere, but I did know he was picking on me.

"If you must know, it was something we all agreed on, well, the majority agreed on it. Everyone senior year thought that we would all be successful in our careers and family, leaving us in a position that was far too busy for us to be bothered about meeting each other every five years or so, so we all decided we'd only have a twenty-year reunion and maybe a fiftieth too. Everyone thought it was the best way to head into the future without looking back. At the time, it seemed like a good idea, but it does seem weird now that you've brought it up. What if we've grown too distant?" I spun up a dish towel I had in hand and snapped it playfully in Sam's direction. He smiled, but didn't really take his attention of his pie. I turned to check the kitchen window for orders, and just happened to catch my Dad staring in our direction with a smile.

"The order for table two will be ready in a minute. You can keep chatting." My Dad grinned as he looked at me and then around me to Sam, who had in the minute decided to look up from his plate, now clean of pie.

Chapter 5

"I knew you would come!" Janet squealed as she saw me walk in the gymnasium doors. "You said you weren't going to come, but you came!" She was past the free-throw line on the gym floor, and came racing my way.

Sam and I stood there, scanning our surroundings, as Janet made her way over to us. The gym was packed with middle-aged folks, all with a drink in hand. There were a few even dancing around the half court line to the REO Speedwagon ballad playing over the loudspeakers. So far it seemed like a pretty lively bunch. Maybe we'd actually have a good time.

"Oh, and who are you?" Janet said in a flirtatious voice, as she held her hand out in front of Sam for him to shake it. "Aren't you a brisk drink of water?" She eyed Sam up and down a few times. One may have been embarrassed by her forwardness, but her pick up line was way more embarrassing, so either Sam didn't know what to aim at, or he just didn't care, because he looked perfectly unscathed. In fact, he seemed to be glowing under the sudden attention. He was eating it up. I looked at him out of the corner of my eye for his reaction, and his smile was taking up the majority of his face. I don't remember him having so many teeth. *Was his smile always this big?* I thought to myself.

"Janet, you remember Sam. He graduated a few years before us. He works for his Dad out on the Howard family land. Don't you remember him? I'm going to give you guys a few to catch up. I'm going to go get a drink, do either of you want anything?" My voice fell onto deaf ears as they were both already in deep conversation and did not take notice to my departure.

I figured I'd use this opportunity to scoot away and let those two chat. Yes, I knew Janet was married, but she was the one that said she wanted to party like we were in high school again. Well, from what I can remember, she was a slut in high school, and maybe that's exactly what Sam needed for a night. After all of Sam and I's flirting, I never felt like we had a sexual tension between us. However, there were times that I thought maybe he wanted more. Maybe Janet was just what he needed to take the edge off, and in the end, take the pressure off of me in thinking he may want something more with me some day. He'd never put the moves on me, but guys just put off a vibe when they are horny, and I have definitely felt his vibes on more than one occasion. I know it's nothing emotional coming from him. He just needs a release, and I'm a woman. If I'm in his company, it's only understandable that he may think he wants me, but he's always been a smart enough gentleman to not cross the line with me. Janet was someone I can see him taking over that line. I'd be more than happy to help him, which was why I was walking away from them just then.

I headed over to the cash bar. I can't even remember the last time I drank. I figured I better play it cool and just go with a glass of white wine. I was never one to be able to hold my liquor very well, and I definitely didn't want to get out of control in front of a bunch of people I haven't seen since my prime. The bartender took my order and poured me a house wine. I fumbled in my pocket book for a few extra dollars to include for the time. In my profession, I know to take care of the servers, regardless if I plan on ordering anymore through the course of the evening. I turned around and looked towards the direction I had left Sam with Janet. I didn't see them. Oh well.

I leaned casually against the bar and drank in my surroundings. I felt like I was at a school dance with the faculty, and I was one of the teachers. We were all so much older. I saw a group at one table that looked like ladies from the old volleyball team. They were laughing it up as a group of men stood close to their table. My guess was it was the husbands, as none of them looked like aged people I knew. Everyone had changed. I felt out of place. I had brought Sam to keep me company, but I couldn't stand in the way of the sparks I saw between him and Janet. I'm sure they would catch up with me later on.

After all, Janet was so excited for her and me to live it up tonight.

"I see you still hate crowds," a voice as alarmingly pleasant as a seasoned sports commentator suddenly took me off my train of thought. I looked up, not prepared to see this absolutely gorgeous man standing right beside me. I felt my knees get weak a little. I stared into his eyes and felt like I was losing my sense of self in a black abyss. The intensity with which he looked at me didn't help me restrain myself at all and it was the soft touch of his arm holding my shoulder that made me realize I seemed to need actual help to stand up in his presence. "Are you okay?" he asked, the sound of his vocals trailed in my ear drum like an echo.

"I'm fine," I finally managed to say, after a pause.

"You look confused, don't you remember?" he asked. So, I did know this fine specimen of a man. How did I know this fine specimen of a man? He obviously wasn't from around town. "Teresa, it's me, Gavin." He seemed a little disappointed in my poor memory, and the sight of his face muscles expressing any sort of discontent made me want to kill myself for causing it, but how could I know? This wasn't the Gavin I remembered.

I looked into his eyes, a daring risk I might add, his presence had already stunted my ability to move around. Eye contact would surely paralyze me entirely. He was Gavin Miller alright. However, he wasn't the Gavin Miller I had shared a pre-calculus class with twenty-five years ago, he was closer to the man I had probably spent a few classes day dreaming about growing up to meet. The irony, it seemed, was that he had been with me all along, waiting to bloom. Gavin had grown into the kind of man that you would focus all your mental energy on whenever you felt down and hopeless and just wanted to dream of a better life. He was the kind of man that you would find running through your mind on a white horse coming to save you from whatever torturous nightmares a maiden was experiencing. The years had been remarkable to him. His face posed no lines and his hair had just the right salt and pepper color that made you question his age, it felt like a mix of wisdom and energetic youth. He was dress to the nines and looked polished from head to toe, almost sparkling. I couldn't believe it was him.

"Gavin. It's so nice to see you." *So nice, I sound so desperate!* I thought to myself. It was all I could think to say. He was virtually making me birth butterflies in my womb which headed to my stomach and made me feel something I hadn't felt for a long time. Here was someone that I had never given a second thought to, crippling me with his mere casual presence. I couldn't believe what he was doing to me, and I immediately began to plot my sweet escape. I was sure that he would pick up on my dreadful composure, as I was beginning to think I wouldn't be able to hold it much longer. If you could call this holding it together.

"You look absolutely ravishing, Teresa. I knew I would have a treat in seeing you if I came back for the reunion." His voice sounded like music, the gentle crystalizing of harmonies not often found together. He owned his voice with such measure that his perfectly broad shoulders and healthy physique made it seem like no one in the world could even hope to speak as eloquently as he was speaking to me right now. As if this wasn't bad enough, he had just given me the most flattering compliment I had ever received.

What was happening? I felt like I was whisked away to a fairytale, and this was happening just by the miracle of his voice and the words coming out of his mouth, his gorgeous chiseled mouth. I knew that I had to get myself together, or he would think that I was swooning over him, excuse me, he would *know* I was swooning over him, which I'm sure was what most females would do in his presence. I had to be different from all these other girls. I hadn't been even remotely interested in a man's looks for so long. Even with regards to Sam, I was aware of what Janet could see in him. He was a nice-looking guy, very wholesome appeal. However, Sam just never was my cup of tea. He just never did it for me. I never got the feeling with Sam, and here I was drowning in that feeling with Gavin.

I took my eyes away from him and focused on the people around us, hoping to regain some self-control.

"Who did you come here with?" he asked, earnestly.

"Oh, uh, I came here with Sam, but he's sort of vanished with Janet for the time being."

"So that leaves you alone?" he teased, a little smile creeping over him.

"I guess. You don't look like you're here with anyone either." I pointed out.

"I just arrived. I drove all the way here. I had a lot on my mind and figured a long drive would help me take the edge off." Hmm, interesting. Gavin had things he needed to take his mind off. Even perfect looking people didn't seem to have perfect lives, but his crisp looking suit suggested his problems weren't all that terrible.

"What's been bothering you?" I asked. I figured if I could keep the attention on him, he wouldn't have time to notice my nervous breakdown, and I feared I wouldn't be able to talk about myself if he asked. Besides, what could I talk about? I spent my days at a diner, nothing happened there.

"Well, since we are at a reunion and everything. I don't feel like my life is where I imagined it would be at this time. So I've been reflecting on that a lot." He had a hint of sadness in his voice, and I felt compelled to hug him and tell him everything would be alright, but of course I didn't, I was still trying to regain control of my motor skills.

I didn't know what else to say so we stood there looking at everyone else for a few more breaths.

"How about you?" he asked. "How's life been treating you?" Great. I had to talk now, and I had to talk about myself.

"Well, I don't really have much to say. You know I'm still at the diner and all, family tradition." I moped. I didn't feel bad about being still at the diner, but my mother's dying wish started to make it a tad bit unfulfilling, especially when I had to acknowledge it out loud.

"I love how you and your family stick together and support each other, my grandparents haven't been very supportive of my choices since I left town. They think I'm turning into some sort of corporate cliché story. At first I didn't mind them, but as the years passed it kind of started to bother me."

"Your grandparents are adorable"

"Yes they are. But their idea of becoming a corporate cliché, or any kind of cliché for that matter, is starting to ring true." He took a sip from his glass after that. He looked as if he was letting all the time that had passed sink in. "I don't really want to sour your mood with mine though. I think I'll just step out for a bit."

"Oh, I can walk you out, I don't really mind." Stupid little me. If he hadn't sensed my pheromones by now, I had just revealed them myself. My woman juices had to be jutting out of my pores onto him with every breath I was taking. What else could drive me to offer my company when he clearly wanted to be alone? I'm sure he was like most men, his first instinct would be to assume I was down for anything.

The worst part about it was that I wasn't sure I wasn't down for anything, especially with a man of his stature.

"That would be great actually, let's get out of here." He said, offering an inviting smile. I made a point to myself to not be that easy. We were going out to talk and that would be it. I didn't have much of a reputation in high school, but I wasn't about to start tonight. It may have been over a year since the last time I fooled around with someone, and I can't even remember his name, as I had made sure it happened during an out-of-town adventure of mine, and only in the heat of the moment, which no one would ever find out about. Single life for a woman in her hometown at my age was grounds for discussion if anyone thought I had been getting lucky. I couldn't go somewhere private with Gavin. Someone might see us leave together. I was the one that had to live in this small town after tomorrow, while everyone else could go back to their dream lives. The last thing I needed was the town gossip to include me losing my regrown cherry over a one night stand with an old classmate.

Perhaps I was overthinking things, Gavin hadn't made any clear advance yet, if anything, he seemed like he wanted to vent with words and not his body. Would that hurt my feelings? If he didn't want to make a move, and just wanted someone to talk to? I started to get cold feet as soon as he took a step forward.

"Wait, I don't think I can leave, Gavin. Sam and Janet might be looking for me," I said as I peered again over the groups of people standing around reminiscing. They were evidently nowhere to be seen, and I blushed a little as I realized how stupid I was making myself look. I came off as a shy teenage girl. I could have told him the real reason that I was afraid of anything happening between us, leaving me with a new whore label in the morning, but I spoke as safely as I could.

He looked a little hurt by this, and strangely, that flattered me a little. "Come on. Just a quick stroll along the grounds. It'd be nice to get away from all this eighties music. High school was great, but the music of that era isn't something I miss. Let's go somewhere quiet. I promise not to bore you with my depression anymore," he said, grabbing my arm and linking it with his. He led me out the side door next to the stage before I could even put up so much as a protest. I had gone from being paralyzed to being a puppet and he had the strings, my body moved automatically wherever he took me. The departure was much less noticeable than walking the entire length of the gym to the front doors. I had forgotten these doors were even here. The doors were perfect for our getaway out into the darkness.

Chapter 6

The tension between us had been slowly raising to a fever pitch, partly because our arms were still linked as we walked down the sidewalk by the playground, and partly because I was running out of things to contribute to our small talk, but mostly because every glance I stole of him overwhelmed me more than the last. Gavin's biceps felt much larger than I remember seeing them as a kid, which was understandable. He had grown into a respectable looking man. I was still a little confused as to how we ended up here together, and what we were doing out there on that chilly October night. Gavin was walking and staring straight forward down the path. He seemed like he was out of small talk topics and was figuring out what to say too.

"What are we doing out here, Gavin?"

I hated to put pressure on him with my question. I would have loved for the moment to be full of pure, unadulterated, romance and the things dreams are made of, but this was becoming a little too weird for me. As I looked up at his face, it was so fashioned for a profile, almost statuesque. Even though I had known him as long as I can remember, I felt I really didn't know him now. He was a stranger that had just whisked me up within a few moments of meeting me, and already had me outside, in the dark without anyone else around. The music was blaring inside. If I had read this scenario incorrectly, no one would hear my calls for help. I wasn't pinning him as a serial killer or anything, but the entire moment had made me paranoid somewhat. This could be a prank that I was paying for years later. Had I done anything to Gavin that I didn't remember? This could play out a million ways. More years had passed that that lifetime we held, and mostly in the eyes of children for us. The last fifteen minutes I had experienced with Gavin were too odd not to question. His angelic presence had gone from bedazzling to unsettling, and his charms were starting to seem more devilish than anything. I had to get some sort of answers, I hoped they would give me some feeling of security.

"I haven't seen you in so long. We've both changed so much. We hardly talked much in high school. What is all of this? Why are we out here?" I pulled my arm out of his and turned towards him. I crossed them in front of my chest, which until this moment had almost been heaving in delight as this handsome man was paying attention to me out of everyone here.

Gavin let out a little laugh, and it caught me off guard. "What's so funny?" I asked.

"Teresa, you really don't remember much, do you?" This just confused me a whole lot more.

"What are you talking about?" I pressed.

"I know we hardly talked much in high school, but I did say something pretty significant after prom, didn't I? But I don't really blame you if you can't remember, we were all a little drunk at the time. I know I wouldn't have had the courage to say anything if I hadn't had that much to drink." He said, rubbing the back of his neck. It was the first sign of insecurity I had seen on him, and it felt so sincere it was heartwarming. And then it hit me, I did recall what he said.

"You said, you had a giant crush on me since the third grade, and you had never had the confidence to tell me until that moment," I didn't want to finish what he said, the last part was far too ridiculous.

"That's not all I said. I said one day, when I had something to offer you. I would come back for you." He said, and my heart froze. It was irrational to think that he had kept his crush on me going for all these years, and it was even more irrational to think that he thought it was worth bringing up right now.

Gavin grabbed my hand and pulled me closer. "Teresa, I have kept up with you all of these years. I ask my grandparents about you all of the time. They told me that they are in your restaurant quite often. Didn't they ever mention it?" He looked me right in the eyes. He sounded so sincere.

He also looked very smooth, and I was falling into the grasp of a fast talker that somehow knew what I wanted to hear. I had never dreamed I would be the object of anyone's crush, and for this length of time – it was borderline obsession. I was scared before, and this was supposed to make it worse, but it didn't. How many women could say they had a deity of a man obsessed with them? I squinted my eyes and stared him up and down. He was smooth. He was oh so smooth. There wasn't one flaw to him. I couldn't fall into his trap without finding out more about where all of this was coming from.

"Teresa, please don't look at me like that," he said, brushing some of my hair back to get a better view of my eyes. "I think about you often. I keep tabs on you by asking my family how you are doing. You're right. We didn't hang out much in high school, but trust me, it wasn't because I didn't want to. You were so intimidating back then. I had no self-esteem and definitely not enough balls to talk much to you, let alone ask you out. Now I have a bit more confidence, and I try not to let opportunities pass me by anymore these days." He shifted his body towards mine, almost touching. I could feel his breath again, and my own started to match his. What this man could do just by breathing into me.

His touch was so soft as he held my hand, even his hands felt rich. He reached for my other one. I looked at him deeply, feeling as though we had been in this eye lock for a while. The romantic version of a stare down. He was the real life version of my knight in shining armor. He stood there, looking into my eyes, oh so intensely. I didn't know what to do. It had been so long since I had felt a man's touch, other than the occasional handshake at the restaurant. The feeling I was getting was tingling in all of the right places. I wanted him to do things to me. I wanted him to do despicable, erotic and dirty things with me, and oh, the things I wanted to do to him. I decided that I'd take a chance. But I didn't have to make the decision or take a chance. It was in that moment that in one movement Gavin wrapped one arm around me and put his other hand on my face, cupping my cheek. Just as I thought he was going in for a romantic kiss, he gently caressed my long hair back and pulled it playfully, but enough to show his dominance in the situation. He deeply kissed my exposed neckline, and then lingered up to my lips. What was happening? I still hadn't gotten my answers, but the electric impulses coursing through the nerves on my neck down to my toes made me care no less. Way less. I needed this, even it wasn't what I had on the agenda for the evening. I deserved to feel good, at least for tonight.

Chapter 7

During high school, the baseball dugout was the designated spot for clandestine make out sessions, and so it seemed natural to head there now. After all, it was our high school reunion, and we were kind of reliving the daring of our youth, or at least the daring we wish we had back then. As we walked across the baseball diamond hand in hand, we looked around to be sure that we were alone, and that nobody else was trying to recapture their youth, it was as deserted as ever, and bathed in darkness, ensuring our privacy.

Gavin led me by the hand into the dugout and we sat next to each other in the darkness, suddenly shy and a little awkward, it really was almost like being a teenager again. A delicious sense of the elicit stole over me and made me bolder than I had even been before. I had not spent much time in the dugouts as a teenager and had always been a bit envious of those who had, it was time to make up for lost time, and dashed hopes.

As Gavin leaned in for a kiss, I reached for his hand, and placed it on my breast. He seemed shocked at first, almost like he didn't know what to do, now that his fantasy was becoming reality. The cold night air and my excitement hardened my nipples under his hand, and seemed to break Gavin's momentary paralysis.

He leaned back in for a kiss as he began kneading my breast, and I wrapped my arms around his neck and drew him to me as I leaned back so that he ended up on top of me and between my legs. I could feel his erection pressing against the now hot and steamy petals of my sex, our clothes making a barrier between us that I couldn't wait to shed.

Gavin began working his hands up under my shirt to get at my bare skin. His hands cupping me and almost burned across my skin, hardening my nipples even more, and sharpening the need coursing through me. I wanted to feel his hot hardness in my hands, so I began fumbling with his belt, urgently trying to get into his slacks.

Taking this as a sign of my willingness, Gavin began his own assault on the buttons of my pants, finally getting them open, he plunged his hand into my panties and found my hot, slippery center, causing me to momentarily forget about getting my hands on his rock hard shaft.

He eased a thick finger into me, the heel of his hand pressing to my clit, and began to slowly pump it in and out of me, priming me for something more. I was so wet and hot that he was soon able to slide a second finger into me, stretching me slightly and making me want to feel him in me. I felt an overwhelming desire to be filled, and to feel his body pressed against me.

I pushed him back to a sitting position and renewed my efforts to free his manhood from his pants. He stood to allow me better access, and I couldn't help but be surprised at the obvious size of the member straining his slacks. I worked his pants and boxers down over hips and his hard cock sprang into view. It was glorious, thick, and long, and his testicles were a heavy sack suspended beneath. He was fairly pulsing with arousal, and when I grasped the base of him and squeezed, he groaned and a pearl of arousal formed on the head. With my other hand, I tested the weight of his sack and leaned forward to taste him. It was such a turn on that he was so incredibly hard for me, but I wanted him dizzy with desire.

I touched my tongue to his tip, tasting his excitement, and he strained forward toward me, allowing me to envelope his ridged head with my mouth. Gavin gasped and thrust his hands into my hair, holding me still until he could get the throbbing of his cock and impending orgasm under control. His breathing was ragged for a moment, and when it evened out, he relaxed his grip on my hair, allowing me to explore his hard length with my lips and tongue.

After a few moments, he reached down to cup my elbows and drew me to my feet, finding my lips with his as he attempted to work my jeans down over my hips. I toed my shoes off, and then helped him to get my pants down, then holding his hand, I laid down on the bench and pulled him to me.

He settled between my thighs, his iron hardness pressed against my molten center, and kissed me as I pressed my hips up, trying to position him to enter me. He drew back, looking me in the eyes, and dragged the tips of his cock down my slit, over my clit, sending a sharp stab of need through me, and placed himself at my opening, as if giving me a chance to change my mind.

There was no way that was happening though, and I wrapped my legs around him and pulled him towards me with my heels, needing to feel him impale me.

His broad head pressed into me slowly, giving me time to accommodate him without pain, but I was so wet that I pulled him in hungrily, his shaft invading me, stretching me, and filling me completely. I took him to the hilt and held him there, relishing the feeling of fullness he was giving me. He began to stroke into me dragging his entire length in and out of me in a rhythm that slowly increased until he was slamming into me and I was thrusting my hips to meet his strokes. Together we detonated, growling, panting and grasping at each other until the waves of pleasure receded, leaving us spent.

Chapter 8

It had been weeks since the reunion. I was laying in my bed trying to get motivated to get ready for the day. Work was starting in a couple of hours, and I didn't want to be racing around in a rush. I wasn't feeling myself lately, I was always tired. This morning was a little different. I almost wondered if I was sick. The wave came over me just then and I jumped from my bed to head to the bathroom. I hugged the toilet as I let out the lasagna I had the night before. I felt disgusting, as I sat on the bathroom floor, wondering if I was going to let out some more. It had been a very long time since I had been sick like this. I couldn't even remember the last time I threw up. Although, in that minute, I felt like the wave in my stomach was making its own tsunami, and it had to come out. I leaned in one more time, and gave out a dry heave. Maybe I would feel better if I took a shower. I took off my robe and started the water.

As I got in the shower, I started to think about the night of the reunion. I hadn't thought much about it over the last few weeks, as I was back in my daily routine. I wasn't even sure why I was thinking of it now. I never saw Gavin after that night, but I didn't think much about it. I also had not seen Janet after that night either. I wasn't surprised in either case. Janet, no doubt, had a one night fling with Sam. I never saw them again after arriving at the reunion. Sam had been in on occasion to the restaurant, but I didn't bring it up, and neither did he. After all, she was a married woman with children. It was something I'm sure no one would ever speak of again.

As for Gavin and I, that night was a surprise, as we had ended up in the back seat of his car shortly after our stroll. Now that I look back at it, I did have fun, and it felt good to be someone's center of attention. I woke up the next day feeling like it had been a dream, a dream that sadly fading away as reality sank in, but I couldn't believe how much I degraded myself as to end up in the back of Gavin's

Escalade. We were grown adults. Most people would have gone home, or to a hotel. We barely got to the car that night. It all seemed as though Gavin's obsession had built up so much over all this time that words failed him and he needed to let it all out with his body before he exploded. After it was all over, we talked very briefly about our distance from one another. He was living in New York City, I had found out during all of this. It was inevitable that it was going to be a one night stand, but at the moment, neither of us really cared. I still didn't. There was something different about this morning though.

As I finished my shower and started to dry off, it dawned on me, I hadn't had my period yet. That was weird, since I have had a schedule almost to the minute since I was a teen. I was only a couple of days late, but my throw up show this morning had me worrying. I finished up and put on some clothes. I opened the vanity doors below the sink and dug around all of the essentials a woman needs. Way back in the back, I found the box I was looking for. I had purchased the pregnancy tests after my trip last year.

I had a scare at that time too. I wasn't one for birth control, so I figured it would catch up with me eventually. I opened up the box, scanning the outside of it for an expiration date. I was in luck, still good. I proceeded to do my business on the stick, and then I waited.

The minutes stood still as I waited for that little stick to tell me my fate. I looked at my phone, one more minute. I counted it down. The numbers seemed to start creeping by. That's when the second line appeared. It was there in front of me. I was pregnant, and there was only one person that could be the father.

Chapter 9

The subsequent months were a blur. I was still working just as much as I ever did. I hadn't told anyone of my pregnancy, and I hadn't started showing yet, so I still had time to hold onto my secret. A lot had happened since I found out I was pregnant, and my emotions were all over the place with my hormones.

My dad had been hospitalized as winter hit. He had come down with pneumonia, and with his age, it had given him a turn for the worse. I was pretty much running the restaurant at this point, but we had cut back on the hours of operation, since Brian was our only other cook at the time.

I was standing at the cash register on a cold November afternoon as the phone rang. I think that I almost felt a bad vibe from the phone before I answered it, although I don't know how that was possible. My head started to spin as I picked up the phone, and I barely managed to get the words out,

"Baxter's Family Restaurant, can I help you?" My voice was hoarse and it cracked.

"Ms. Baxter. It's Dr. Mitchell. I'm sorry to be the bearer of bad news this afternoon but we need you to come down to the hospital. Your father's condition has worsened and he is in a critical condition. We are doing everything we can to help him, but I would advise you to come over and help him get his affairs in order."

It was the worst possible thing that I could have heard in that moment. Everything went black and I was out.

***

It took me more than a few moments of consciousness to figure out that I was lying in a hospital bed next to my father. I looked over at him, and he seemed to be awake, so in a very raspy voice, I tried to get his attention. "Dad, are you there?"

He turned over to look at me, I could tell he needed a lot of effort to do that. He gave a terribly weak smile, then spoke "Would you look at us? We should just let Brian take over the family restaurant."

I gave a weak laugh, we were both a sight for sore eyes. "I'm pregnant, Dad." His eyes opened wide, and he seemed to be in shock. I gave him another smile, telling him I was happy I was going to give him a grandson. He tried to speak, but he suddenly went into a spasm of coughs. He started to have trouble breathing and I gathered up all my strength to sit up and start shouting for a nurse. Just then he mustered all the energy he had to say one last thing, "Take care of my grandkid. Explore the world." Then he deeply breathed out, and that was it. Dad was gone. Brian and Patricia had just shown up from outside, as they had drove me after I passed out back at the restaurant. When they realized what was happening, they started to cry. I was crying too. It was one of the worsts days of my life, as you can imagine.

"Teresa, may I speak with you?" Dr. Mitchell had entered the room. He looked concerned, and now that Dad was gone, I couldn't begin to imagine what bad news he had to tell me now.

I looked at my Dad's body. I didn't want to leave his side just yet. "Can this wait, Doctor?" I asked, thinking whatever it was could wait.

"I'm afraid not, Teresa. Please come with me, this will only take a moment." Dr. Mitchell turned and exited the room. It was obvious this was terribly urgent and confidential, so I got up and followed him with the little energy I had.

"What is it, Doctor?" I asked after finding him out in the hallway waiting for me.

"Teresa, I didn't want to say this in front of the others, but I have to let you know that the baby is fine. You had a very substantial fall this afternoon, and I want you to know that we did all the necessary checks, and everything seems fine. However, I highly recommend you take it easy. With the pregnancy, and your father, and the business, the stress might get to you. You need a break from this. You need to relax, or you are going to have complications with this pregnancy. Do you understand?"

Dr. Mitchell came over with his wife to the diner every other Tuesday and Thursday. He meant well as he spoke, and passed on his condolences as he left. I leaned against the wall, trying to take it all in. My mind was racing, and my tears were still falling. I felt heavy, and my weak body felt like it couldn't handle anything at the moment. I hadn't thought about the baby's condition since I came to, and after what had just transpired, all I could think about was being with my dad on his deathbed. I had thought about the phone call and the news that made me pass out, and now the doctor was reminding me that I had this pregnancy to worry about. Thank goodness Dr. Mitchell didn't ask who the father was. I had managed to keep all of this a secret up until now. I didn't need the entire population of this little town knowing that I was carrying a bastard child. I had to find a way out. My father's last words echoed my mother's last wish. I needed to get away or I would lose my mind, or worse, my child. I made up my mind in that moment that I would leave town after Dad's affairs were wrapped up. I was going to build a new life for me and my unborn child.

Chapter 10

Everyone was in the diner. Brian had come up with the idea of having everyone over after the burial to honor the memory of my Dad's legacy, so everyone came. It had been a long while since the diner had been this full. None of the faces were unfamiliar, but everyone preferred coming in on their own days, at their own time, according to their own frequency. This was a rare moment in which they all had to come over at once.

Brian wanted me to take it easy and rest a little, knowing I had just come out of the hospital but I couldn't rest, we were at a full capacity. I had to help out.

"Order up!" it sounded so peculiar, hearing Brian say it and I felt like it was further confirmation that I had to leave this place.

I immediately stood up and tugged on my uniform. I hadn't gotten around to ordering any new uniforms, life had simply been too fast paced for me, and now I feared my baby bump might start to show. I wouldn't be needing that new uniform anymore, so I brushed the thought to the back of my head. This was technically my last working day at Baxter's Family Restaurant.

I grabbed the two plates out of the window, where Brian stood behind with a worried look on his face. I wondered how he would take the news when I told him I was leaving, but I quickly brushed it to the back of my head, one problem at a time. Brian had recreated Dad's *Masterpiece Meatloaf* for the day's special board, and the sample I had was pretty close to Dad's recipe. I told Brian that my Dad would be proud, and it wasn't just to flatter him, it was pretty honest. I turned around with the plates in-hand and headed to the table.

It was Dr. Mitchell, and he was with his wife. The glare he gave me suggested that he disapproved of me working in my current condition, but the look Mrs. Mitchell gave me suggested he hadn't acknowledged the doctor-patient confidentiality I thought we had entirely.

"Here's your order," I said as I placed the plates in front of them. "Enjoy your meal, this was Dad's special!" I gave them a smile, and quickly started to make my way back.

"Teresa!" the voice that called me stopped me in my tracks. I turned to where the voice had come from and saw who it was. It had come from table seven, the Martin's favorite table in the Restaurant, and for the first time in years, they had shown up with Gavin. I gulped, nervous, and made my way to their table.

"Hello everyone," I greeted them all. "How may I help you guys?"

"Oh we've already made our orders. I think Gavin here is just a little bit impatient and wants to talk to you," Phyllis said, giving me a knowing smile. I looked at Gavin, and all he could say was, "Guilty as charged." With a cool smile. I could not believe how insensitive this guy could be in such a situation. Why was he back in town? Was it for the funeral?

"Oh, okay. I'll have to see you a little later, I'm kind of busy right now." I said, gesturing to the entire restaurant.

"Oh, sure. No problem, I'm around until tomorrow and I just felt that we should catch up. I am staying with my parents and I figured I could see you later on. My condolences, by the way." He offered.

"Thanks. I'm sure we can figure something out." I said, and practically ran away. It must have been the hormones again, or the fact that my father had just been buried, or the fact that this was my last day at a restaurant I had spent my entire life at, and that I didn't even know where I was going and what I was going to do when I got there, or the fact that I was a single mother and my baby daddy was in the restaurant and wanted to 'hang out' later, but I ended up in the bathroom stall crying for a long time.

＊

"Why do you have so many tattoos?" I asked.

It was later in the day and my hormones and emotions had calmed down. Okay, they hadn't really calmed down, but they were flaring up in an entirely different way now. I was back home, and Gavin was with me.

"I don't know, I got one when I was younger and I went into a sort of phase and ended up getting a lot more," he replied, but the way he suddenly looked away while talking made me feel like he was holding something back. A secret about his past maybe.

"Thanks for helping me close up the restaurant and everything. It's been a really a long day," I said, forking at the meat loaf I had taken home from the restaurant, courtesy of yours truly, Brian.

"Don't worry about it, it's not like I had anything better to do with my time." Gavin said. His choice of words offended me a little, it made me feel like I was something he does when his bored, not because he was compelled to. We hadn't communicated at all since our last encounter, and now the air was thick with unspoken words. I hadn't told him about the baby yet, I didn't know how to and I didn't even know if I wanted to tell him. I had a lot of decisions to make about the baby and where we were going to end up, but I felt like if I told him, he would throw himself at us and I would find myself right in the middle of a life I was unsure of. I had to find my own footing first, maybe then I would feel comfortable telling him.

I was in an awkward place as things were. I was suffering from the post-funeral syndrome, where everyone was gone and now it had just had to be you and your thoughts of your lost loved one. I couldn't bear to be alone in that moment, and so Gavin's next words were golden. "Listen, if you don't want to be alone tonight, I can hang around. My flights tomorrow and I won't get in your way at all, I could even sleep on the couch."

"I would love that." I said quickly, looking him straight in the eyes. I hoped I didn't come off as needy, but I really couldn't bear to be alone just yet. I needed some company. "I mean, if it isn't a bother to you." I added, looking away.

"Of course it isn't," he said, moving closer to me. "I know you must really be hurting right now and it isn't good for you to be alone." We readjusted our sitting positions and I found myself with my head on his lap.

The feelings I started to experience made me feel rather guilty, as we made small talk, all I could think about was how amazing our sexual encounter had actually been. I had never felt the way Gavin made me feel that night, never in my entire life. If anything could distract me from my thoughts right now, it would be his touch, but I felt self-conscious having buried my father only hours earlier, and the baby in my womb would add to my worries, but don't pregnant people have sex in safe positions? I would have to limit him to a few positions, tell him I wasn't feeling well. Why was I thinking like this? What if he wasn't even feeling the same way?

"I've really missed you," he said, stroking my hair, and I immediately knew he felt the same way. This time I would make the first move. I got up from his chest and pressed my lips against his, and the heat immediately ignited just as it had before.

We were groping at each other furiously and shedding clothes at record speed. In no time, we were naked and wrapped around each other, desperate to be joined together, unable and unwilling to slow down to savor the moment. He used his mouth to nip at me and kiss his way down my body until he found my swollen clit, lashing me with his tongue until I was drowning him in my juices as an orgasm pounded through me, leaving me hoarse from my cries of ecstasy.

Then he rose up between my still trembling thighs, his face still glistening with my honey, and impaled me with his cock in one smooth stroke, tearing a gasp from me. Like animals we rutted, my fingernails scoring his back and buttocks, and his fingers digging into my hips as he thrust into me. He filled me so completely with every thrust, stretching me around his thick base that I was pushed immediately to the brink of another earth shattering orgasm. Simultaneously we screamed out our release, and collapsed in exhaustion, his weight pressing me into the cushions of my couch, and we slept that way, holding each other the rest of the night.

Chapter 11

As I stood outside the boardroom, an overwhelming rush came over me. What was I doing here? How could I ever think, as an older, pregnant, single woman, that I could try to enter the world of Corporate America after all of these years, and without any kind of experience? And why did I choose New York to enter this life, instead of gradually moving up from the small hometown I had loved? My sink or swim attitude had done this to me. I had to stand beside my choices. I had done my best to prepare, but the days leading up to this meeting were not forgiving enough for me to learn an entirely new career. I had to go with what I had, and that was unnerving.

Could I throw them off of my lack of experience by dressing and acting the part? It was worth a shot, right? I had spent the last few days looking for the perfect outfit and accessories for this meeting. I wasn't sure that I had gotten it right. Just then, I caught my reflection in the window beside me. I had to admit that I did dress the part. I could pass as a businesswoman. I stood there wearing a navy-blue hand-me-down Chanel suit from my sister. The tailoring of the suit made it fit me in a way that made me think the seamstress had a vision of my curves when designing it. Even my sister couldn't deny having to part with it after seeing me try it on. I had paired the outfit with my classic nude pumps, which I consider my "Power Shoes," giving me a few more inches and making me feel more powerful. All in all, my appearance was the one thing I was confident about. Time had been pretty good to me, and my looks.

The large door to my fate was right in front of me. The hallway was freezing, and it was not helping me to call down as I tried to get all of the butterflies out of my stomach. It was pure torture. What were these people going to say when they find out that the only experience on my resume was working as a waitress for my father at the family restaurant? Over the years waiting tables, I had spent countless hours daydreaming about what it would be like to be a businesswoman working in an office. Here I was, at the beginning of the road in my daydream, and I was terrified.

I thought about the comfort of the restaurant, and how I had stayed to help with the family business, because it was safe and comfortable... and what I knew best. I was far from my hometown of Muleshoe, Texas, and the culture of the big city was extremely overwhelming. After all of the years of staying in my hometown, I thought about how I had stayed because I knew deep down that my father enjoyed spending our work days together, as did I. I always wanted to be there for him, but I had never imagined what it would be like when he wasn't there for me. Now here I was, alone, trying to find the career I was determined to have.

These executives are going to eat me alive. I had to get my shit together. I had no choice, but to go through with this interview and hope for the best. With Dad's passing, and the selling of his business, this was my chance, my chance to make something of myself. It was the chance to stop wondering, and just do it. It all had to start somewhere, and it was going to start with this meeting, in this boardroom.

The chill from the eighth-floor air conditioning vent blew heavily on my neck, offering a feeling of relief as my sweat started to dry. I had to go in. I looked at my watch, 9 o'clock on the dot. They would be expecting me. I tugged my jacket down to relieve the garment of any slightly wrinkles, and grabbed the door handle. I've got this, I thought. It's now or never.

Entering the room, which was even colder than the hallway, I gazed around, not prepared for what was in-store. Around the table sat a handful of people, all younger than me, and definitely dressed better than me. The gaze of their eyes on me as I stood there, had me wonder if they could see the fear in my face. It was hard to imagine them as executives, as some of them could have been young enough to be a kid of mine, in another life. What had I gotten myself into? The ridicule I was preparing myself to accept was keeping me from being completely aware of my surroundings.

It was then that I saw a dark figure in the corner of the room, looking out the window, with his hands in his pockets. It was difficult to see the details of his features, as he stood in the shadow. His stature said it all though. He stood much taller than the average man: and he stood proud. He gazed out on the city, and even with his back to the group, he gave off the feeling of having power over everyone in his presence. As he heard the door close behind me, he turned, and I realized... it was him. It was Gavin.

Chapter 12

After the interview, which I have to say that I rocked, Gavin asked me to wait for him outside. After a few short moments he joined me in the hallway, took my arm, and we walked to the lobby. He explained to me that he had arranged for the interview as a way to entice me to move to New York.

"I arranged the interview", he said, "but it's up to the board whether they want to hire you or not. I didn't want you to feel like you got the position based on our relationship, and if you are hired, you won't be working directly for me."

"I wasn't aware that we had a relationship." I said.

"That's what I'm trying to tell you Teresa, I want to be part of your life."

"It's not just about us," I said, "it's more complicated than that."

"What could possibly make it more complicated?" He said. "I love you Teresa, I have for a very long time and I know it's probably a shock to you, but all I've ever wanted was you, a life together, and hopefully a family. I have everything, success, money, a home, but it all means nothing to me if I don't have you to share it with."

I couldn't hide the emotion that his words evoked in me, they gave me hope that I wasn't going to be alone, that I could have love, a career, and a family. Did he really mean all of this though? There was only one way to find out, so with a tear sliding down my cheek, I looked up at him and said the words that I was scared to death would send him running in the other direction. "Gavin, I'm pregnant."

The shock on his face almost sent me bolting away, but I held my breath, waiting for him to process the information that had just been dropped on him out of the blue. Slowly, the look on his face transformed to something more hopeful.

"You're sure?" He whispered

I nodded, unable to speak, and afraid to look at him, "Since the first time we were together."

Tears gathered at the corners of his eyes, his face lit with a joyful smile, and he slid his arms around me, "I'm going to be a father!" He exclaimed quietly.

Gavin's happiness at the news gave me real hope for the first time, and I finally believed that it could all work out.

"Excuse me, Sir?" One of the women from the interview approached Gavin, "May I speak to you a moment?

Gavin stepped away and they had a brief conversation before he returned to her with an ecstatic look on his face. "The position is yours. If you still want it..."

***

It's been a year now, and everything has worked out even better than I had hoped. I started my new career, and while it wasn't easy, I have been steadily working my way up the ladder.

Gavin Jr. was born healthy, and he has two happy parents, that were married shortly after he was born. You could say I've had my Boss's baby...

*****
THE END